# DISENCHANTED

ROBERT KROESE

# DISENCHANTED

47NORTH

Text copyright © 2012 Robert Kroese
All rights reserved.
Printed in the United States of America.
No part of this book may be reproduced, or stored in a retrieval system,
or transmitted in any form or by any means, electronic, mechanical,
photocopying, recording, or otherwise, without express written permis-
sion of the publisher.

Published by 47North
P.O. Box 400818
Las Vegas, NV 89140

ISBN-13:9781612185422
ISBN-10: 1612185428
Library of Congress Control Number: 2012953722

For Speed Pony

# One

By most accounts, Boric the Implacable was, while he was alive, an incomparable badass. By all accounts, he was an even bigger badass after he died.

For most people,[1] death marks the end of one's career, whether that career is baking bread, blowing glass, or—as in Boric's case—hacking other people to pieces with a sword. But for Boric, death was just another bullet point on his already impressive ass-kicking résumé.

Whether death improved Boric overall is a matter of some debate, but there's little question that it enhanced him professionally. In addition to his already impressive catalog of badassery, death granted him invulnerability, the importance of which can't be overstated in Boric's chosen profession. There were some negatives, of course, but even these could often be turned to his advantage: those who were not convinced to surrender by rumors of his combat prowess and invulnerability could be compelled to yield when they caught a whiff of his rotting-cabbage-mixed-with-rancid-bacon odor. Still, he couldn't deny his relief when the flesh still doggedly clinging to his bones began to desiccate, leaving him smelling more like the attic of an old farmhouse and less like a can of beef stew that has quietly gone bad in a forgotten corner of the farmhouse's pantry.

---

1    All of them, at last count.

Boric's birth was unremarkable, being only the first of many experiences involving a vagina, lots of friction and grunting, and the copious secretion of bodily fluids. His death, on the other hand, was quite interesting. It happened like this:

Boric the Implacable needed a new coat. As the King of Ytrisk, a middling kingdom composed of six nearly forgotten provinces cobbled together at the periphery of the Old Realm, Boric generally got what he wanted, and in this case what he wanted was a coat that would keep him from freezing to death while walking from his bedroom to his throne room. Like most medieval castles, Kra'al Brobdingdon was designed to keep out every enemy except the unsleeping chill that had, in fact, killed more of the citizens of Ytrisk than all of its foreign enemies combined. Boric therefore commissioned the weaving of the Warmest Coat in All Ytrisk. Some three months after he had issued the command, just when the icicles hanging from Brobdingdon Tower had begun the maddening *drip, drip, drip* that signaled the end of winter, just when Boric had all but forgotten about the Warmest Coat in All Ytrisk, four of the royal weavers appeared in his throne room, bearing something that Boric at first mistook for an emaciated bear.

In fact it was the Warmest Coat in All Ytrisk, and it lived up to its name. Within minutes of putting it on—or, more accurately—crawling inside of it, Boric was sweating something fierce. Despite the fact that he could see his own breath, the throne room seemed to have become suddenly, oppressively warm. Every beat of his heart sent out waves of heat that were then corralled mercilessly by the coat and sent hurling back at him. It was like being baked alive in a loaf of bread. Boric nodded in approval. This was indeed the Warmest Coat in All Ytrisk. In fact, it was probably the Warmest Coat in All the Old Realm and quite possibly in the Uncivilized Wastes of the North as well.

Then the itching started.

The outside of the coat was made of wild mink and the liner inside was fine silk stitched over cotton. The bulk of the coat, however, was the finest Ytriskian wool. Ytriskian wool was renowned in all Dis for its warmth, its durability, and, most of all, its excruciating itchiness. It didn't matter that Boric had a layer of clothing and a two-layered lining between his skin and the Ytriskian wool; trying to ward off the itchiness of Ytriskian wool with a few layers of fabric was like trying to frighten a wolf with a daffodil. The insidious, wiry tendrils of Ytriskian wool clawed through the fabric until they reached Boric's warm, soft flesh and began to itch it.

The itching started in his chest and rapidly spread to his armpits and then down his sides and over his shoulders. Once it had engulfed his entire back, it shot down his arms. Even his hands, which were uncovered, and his lower legs, which were encased in leather boots, began to itch in sympathy with the rest of his body. It was unbearable.

"Get it off!" he howled in a regrettably unmonarchical manner. "It itches! Get it off!"

The royal weavers struggled to extricate him from the mass of fabric, finally collapsing in a sweaty heap in the throne room, with the Warmest Coat in All Ytrisk threatening to smother them en masse.

Boric tore off his clothing and spent several minutes scratching every inch of his skin. At last he spoke. "What is the meaning of this?"

The head of the royal weavers got to his feet. "Sire, it is the finest in Ytriskian wool. Unmatched in warmth, durability, and, unfortunately, itchiness." He walked to a window. "Behold, your highness. The Ytriskian sheep."

Boric glanced out the window. Kra'al Brobdingdon was located at the edge of the city, overlooking the treacherous but verdant hills to the north. Following the head weaver's gesture, he located a grassy knoll strewn with rocks. Some fifty sheep occupied the knoll. Half of them were eating while the other half appeared to be rolling about on the rocks in a very unsheeply manner.

"By Varnoth," muttered Boric in dismay. "What are those sheep doing?"

"They are itching," the head weaver replied. "Centuries ago, the Ytriskian shepherds were instructed to breed the sheep with the Warmest Wool in All Ytrisk. As you see, they succeeded. However, no other considerations were taken into account, and today the Ytriskian wool is so itchy that even the sheep can hardly stand to wear it."

As Boric watched, one of the sheep stood at the edge of a crevice, its dim sheep eyes surveying the gap, its small sheep brain weighing its options. After a few seconds, the sheep gave a short bleat and then leapt into the chasm below. Boric could have sworn that he saw a look of relief on the sheep's face.

"This shall not stand," growled Boric. "What of the Peraltic wool?"

"The Peraltians have stopped trading with us," said the head weaver. "They are allied with the Skaal, who as you know are still upset over our trade agreement with the Blinskians."

"Is that so?" asked Boric, rubbing his beard with his fingers.

$$\Sigma$$

Three days later, the Kingdom of Ytrisk was at war with the Kingdom of Skaal. As any historian will tell you, wars tend to be the result of any number of complex socioeconomic and political factors, but to the extent that this war could be said to be about anything, it was about the Itchiest Coat in All Ytrisk.[2] The nominal goal of the war was

---

2  It is also said that history is written by the victors. This was particularly true in the Old Realm, where the official historians at the Library of Avaress had been required for centuries to be named Victor.

to take control of Kra'al Weibdrung, a poorly insulated observation tower in the Dagspaal Mountains just over the River Ytrisk, which marked the uneasy border between the Kingdom of Ytrisk and the Kingdom of Skaal. From Kra'al Weibdrung, the Skaal could see what the Ytriskians in northern Ytrisk were up to, which at any moment was mostly trying to keep their sheep from committing suicide.

Still, the Ytriskians resented this lookout tower, considering it an incursion on their territory. Boric the Implacable was determined to oust the Skaal from Kra'al Weibdrung because it would demonstrate to all the Old Realm that the Ytriskians weren't going to take their shit anymore. And once Ytrisk had demonstrated its non-shit-taking-ness, the Peraltians might rethink their alliance with the Skaal, or at least occasionally overlook it and send a few nonsuicidal sheep their way. Anyway, that was the plan.

Unfortunately, Kra'al Weibdrung was an eighty-foot tower with sheer rock walls. It had one entrance, which was only accessible by scaling a two-hundred-foot cliff in full view of the famed Archers of Kra'al Weibdrung, who were known for being able to skewer a sheep from three hundred yards.[3] Kra'al Weibdrung was, for all practical purposes, impenetrable. The only way to take Kra'al Weibdrung was to cut off the Skaal supply route and wait for the archers to die of starvation. And that's exactly what Boric the Implacable and his retinue of soldiers did.

The Skaal, for their part, weren't about to try to send supplies up a two-hundred-foot cliff; it was hard enough to keep the tower supplied when nobody was trying to kill them. The Skaal realized shortly after they'd finished building Kra'al Weibdrung that they

---

3 This actually only happened once, and isn't as impressive as it sounds. When you've got a dozen bored archers at the top of a tower overlooking a pasture occupied by some six thousand sheep, it's only a matter of time before a sheep gets skewered. Additionally, one witness claimed that the sheep deliberately moved into the path of the arrow.

had made a terrible mistake: the fort was nearly impossible to keep supplied and in any case taught them nothing about the Ytriskians other than the fact that their sheep were seriously troubled. They'd have been glad to desert Kra'al Weibdrung if it weren't for the loss of face that would ensue. The Skaal archers, knowing that no supplies were forthcoming, decided to take the offensive.

The two hundred or so Skaal who had been walled up in the tower rappelled down the cliff under the cover of night. They took cover and the next morning their crack archers shot volley after volley of arrows at the two hundred or so Ytriskian aggressors, who waited a hundred yards across the plain. The archers, being accustomed to shooting from great altitudes at large, slow-moving, easy-to-spot animals with brains the size of tangerines and almost no will no live, found their skills wanting against the men across the field wearing metal shirts. The men in metal shirts, for their part, quickly tired of having their metal shirts dented by arrows and charged.

The Skaal didn't stand a chance. Besides being out of practice at anything other than playing cards and firing arrows into sheep, they had as their leader a cowardly imbecile by the name of Captain Randor. It had been Captain Randor's idea to advance on the Ytriskian belligerents, but once the battle started, he was nowhere to be found. In contrast, Boric the Implacable led the Ytriskian charge with a battle cry that struck fear into the hearts of the Skaal warriors—even the one who had once skewered a sheep from three hundred yards. The Ytriskians slaughtered half the Skaal and disarmed the remainder, sending them home to report to King Sharvek in Skaal City about the fall of Kra'al Weibdrung.

Boric handpicked a contingent of his most expendable soldiers to man the tower of Kra'al Weibdrung, and together they scaled the cliff wall. The men waited at the foot of the tower while Boric climbed to the top of the tower to address them. He walked to the edge of the parapet and began, "Brave men of Ytrisk—"

He had intended his address to be somewhat more comprehensive than this but was forced to cut it short, having been stabbed between the ribs with a broadsword. Captain Randor, it seemed, had been hiding under a pile of rubbish at the rear of the tower and had been compelled by his cowardly and imbecilic brain to stab Boric the Implacable in the back. Captain Randor was one of the few who had not yet heard what a stupendous badass Boric was. That was about to change.

Boric spun around, blood spewing from fresh gashes in both his chest and his back. He calmly drew his sword, took two steps toward Randor and sliced his head clean off. Randor's head and body fell separately to the cold stone floor, with a *thud!* and a *tink!*

This latter surprised Boric. Military men were supposed to *thud!* or *clank!* to the ground. Only sedentary nobles and merchants *tink!*ed.

Boric, feeling dizzy and light-headed, shambled toward Randor's corpse, which was still making an impressive effort to pump blood to Randor's head. His head unfortunately lay some three feet away—an insurmountable distance for even the most robust circulatory system. Wheezing and coughing up blood, Boric felt underneath the corpse, finding a small cloth purse full of coins. He tore the purse from Randor's belt, spilling its contents on the stone: forty gold coins. Boric's mind reeled: setting aside the fact that no soldier would carry that much money into battle, no soldier would *have* that much money, period. Each of those coins represented a month's wages for a Skaal captain.

Before he could fully analyze the situation, Boric fell to the cold stone floor, dead. Boric's reputation as a badass unmarred by the desperate final act of a cowardly imbecile, his spirit readied itself for its journey to the Hall of Avandoor, where he would enjoy an eternal banquet with the other stupendous badasses throughout history. He hoped to sit next to Greymaul Wolfsbane or, in a pinch,

Hollick the Goblin-Slayer. On second thought, Hollick the Goblin-Slayer seemed, from what Boric knew, to be the sort who would hog all the mead. Boric would insist on sitting near Greymaul. Surely his slaying of the Ogre of Chathain twenty years earlier, if not the decapitation of Randor, had earned him that much.

Boric couldn't hear the shouts of the men below, who didn't realize he was dead and were nervously handing him possible lines for his speech. "I salute you for your brave, uh, service to Ytrisk," one of them offered. "I declare this a national holiday with, um, free beer," another suggested. "And dancing girls!" shouted a third.

All Boric heard were the haunting cries of a Wyndbahr—one of the great, white, winged bears that served as steeds to the Eytriths—the spirits who escorted warriors to the hallowed Hall of Avandoor. The Wyndbahr alighted with a thump on the stone floor next to Boric, its giant, bird-like wings pushing powerful gusts of wind over Boric. The Eytrith leapt from its back. She was a fierce-looking woman, tall and beautiful, and bathed in a sort of bluish-gray light. She wore fine-meshed chainmail and a silvery breastplate that made her cleavage into an inviting crevasse between two vast, snow-covered hills. Her blond hair was braided in a ponytail that reached her waist.

"Boric of Ytrisk," she intoned, "thou hast been summoned to the Hall of Avandoor!"

"Kick *ass*," Boric replied, unable to contain his enthusiasm. Wondering if there was a rule against fraternizing with the Eytriths, he got to his feet.

Actually, his feet remained exactly where they were; his spirit was now standing over his body, regarding the pierced husk of flesh with some derision. "Good riddance!" he said, giving himself a kick in the ribs. He was surprised to see the corpse jerk in response to the blow.

"Boric! There is no time to lose!" the Eytrith hissed. "Thou must mount the Wyndbahr!" She was already back on top of the great winged beast.

"Right," said Boric. "Mount the Wyndbahr." He moved toward the creature, but something was holding him back.

"Be not afraid," said the Eytrith, patting the creature on the neck. "He biteth not."

"Afraid!" howled Boric. "Boric the Implacable fears no creature on Earth or in heaven! I just can't seem to…"

The problem, it was becoming clear, was that Boric had died clutching his sword, and his brain had never had a chance to issue the order to release his grip. Boric, the spirit, was holding the sword as well. While death had broken the connection between Boric's flesh and spirit, the flesh-hand and spirit-hand still overlapped on the hilt of the sword, and now he was playing tug-o-war over the sword with his own corpse.

"Thou will have to drop the sword," said the Eytrith.

"Drop my sword!" cried Boric. "A warrior does not enter the Hall of Avandoor unarmed!"

"We can get you a new sword," said the Eytrith, dropping her formal tone. "Seriously. We need to go. I've got six more warriors to deliver today. If I show up late, they start wandering around, scaring the shit out of people. And if they wander too far, I can't find them, and I get behind schedule. Please, for Grovlik's sake, just drop the sword!"

Boric was stubbornly attempting to pry the sword from his cold, dead fingers. "Damn you," he growled at himself. "Let go!"

But Boric the Implacable was as stubborn in death as he was in life, and he wasn't about to surrender his sword—not even to his own spirit. For this was no ordinary sword: it was one of the seven Blades of Brakboorn—designed by the Elves of Quanfyrr, forged by the Dwarves of Brun, and blessed by the Gnomes of Swarnholme.[4] This sword, known as Brakslaagt, was the blade that slew the Ogre

---

4  This last didn't add any value to the sword, but Boric had been in the area and the Gnomes of Swarnholme liked to bless things.

of Chathain, minced the Trolls of Trynsvaan, and banished many a chunk of salted pork that had been stuck between Boric's molars. He wasn't about to leave it to be buried with this pathetic meatsack.

The spirit of Boric tried slamming the corpse's fist against the stone, stomping on his fingers, even biting his knuckles in an attempt to get it to release the sword, all to no avail. The corpse simply wouldn't let go.

Voices could be heard from the stairwell leading to the tower. The men had evidently figured out something was wrong and were making their way up to Boric. If they were to emerge from the stairwell now, they would be greeted with the bizarre sight of Boric the Implacable's otherwise flaccid corpse waving a sword wildly in the air with its outstretched right arm.

"Boric! Let go of the sword!" growled the Eytrith. "This is your last chance! Come now or remain here, cursed to roam the plains of Dis as a wraith!"

"Fine," muttered Boric, and released his grip on the hilt. But the sword remained in his hand.

"Boric!" growled the Eytrith again.

"I'm trying!" Boric snapped, beginning to feel the slightest inkling of something like fear. His fingers seemed to be stuck to the sword, as if they were frozen in a block of ice. He had no more luck prying his immaterial fingers off the hilt than he had with the corpse's.

"It's stuck!" he cried to the Eytrith. "I can't get my hand off the sword!"

"Well, thou canst not take it with thee," announced the Eytrith. "Perhaps," she added after a moment, "the sword is cursed?"

"Oh," said Boric, remembering something that he had very nearly succeeded in forgetting over the past twenty years. "Oh, shit."

# Two

When the Old Realm finally collapsed under the weight of its own superlative wondrousness, it left behind a ragtag collection of city-states and quasi-independent fiefdoms that fought like wild dogs over the scraps of the Realm's bloated carcass. For the average peasant, the end of the Realm was just another reason for things to go to shit. The marauding bandits that had been kept more or less in check by the vague threat of being drawn and quartered by Soldiers of the Realm now roamed freely, raping and pillaging whomever and whatever there was to rape and pillage. Many of the Soldiers of the Realm, who were no longer getting paid on a regular basis, joined in the raping and pillaging as well.

For a brave, resourceful young man like Boric, the chaos presented an opportunity. His father, Toric, had been a wealthy landowner who had begrudgingly paid tribute to the Overlord of the Realm in the distant capital of Avaressa, but when it became clear that Avaressa had become preoccupied with defending itself from the goblins to the east, he withheld his tribute and focused on building an alliance with the petty chieftains in Ytrisk. Toric became the Duke of Ytrisk in defiance of the weakened Realm. After the Realm fell, he had himself crowned King of Ytrisk. Other provinces in the region reacted to the threat of a united Ytrisk by forming their own ad hoc realms—the Peraltians to the east and the Skaal to the south, the Blinskians to the southeast, and beyond Blinsk the Quirini. Avaressa itself was reduced to being the capital of Avaress—now just another of the Six Kingdoms of Dis.

In retrospect, Boric's ascension to King of Ytrisk may seem to have been assured by his circumstances, but that is far from the truth. For one thing, Boric was the youngest of the three sons of Toric, which doomed him to a tertiary role in the Dukedom of Ytrisk. In fact, his father had it in his head to send Boric to the dismal, rocky island of Bjill, some three miles off Ytrisk's western coast, to oversee the lucrative pumice mines there. Overseeing Ytrisk's pumice supply was a vital task in the Kingdom of Ytrisk, but it wasn't a job with a lot of potential for upward mobility. Additionally, most inhabitants of Bjill succumbed within a few years to a form of gradual, creeping pneumonia known simply as the "Bjills." Bjill's low-grade volcanic activity, combined with its location smack in the middle of a ringlet of tall, uninhabitable atolls that arrested nearly all air movement, gave it an atmosphere that was simply too cool, damp, and filled with microscopic crud for mammalian lungs to operate for any extended period of time. Bjill had a single, eternal season characterized by temperatures that lingered halfway between brisk and freezing, and a featureless sky that alternated between dismal gray and black. Only suicide killed more Bjillians than the Bjills.

Boric's opportunity to escape a death sentence on Bjill came in the form of a wild ogre[5] who wandered down from the Chathain Mountains one day to wreak havoc in southern Ytrisk.

Now the problem with ogres is that they are bullies, and despite being notoriously dim, they have an uncanny ability to know when

---

5  The designation of this particular ogre as "wild" should not be taken to mean that most ogres are tame. In fact, nearly all attempts to domesticate the ogre have failed. The use of "wild" here is more akin to its use in the phrase "a wild hair," i.e., one that has appeared where you'd rather not have one.

they are outclassed. An ogre isn't going to attack a garrison of soldiers or, for that matter, a troll or even a bugbear. Ogres pick their victims carefully, and they are masters of the hit-and-run. Ogres like to hide in caves and drop rocks on passing merchants or feast on errant goats. After the attack, the ogre will skedaddle out of the area and find a new place with easy pickings. He isn't going to hang around waiting for somebody to be a hero.

This particular ogre, who went by the name Skoorn, was (by ogreish standards) exceedingly clever, and he had developed a taste for what ogres call "screech melons." Screech melons were small, juicy, pinkish fruits that could often be found in the dwellings of humans. The humans loved their screech melons, taking great pains to keep them from spoiling or being bruised. The humans kept the melons wrapped in cloths and generally stored them in little padded cages, taking them out only occasionally to clean them or perform other screech melon maintenance that was beyond the understanding of ogres. Despite the humans' devotion to their melons, it was often a simple matter for an ogre to reach through an open window, pluck the melon from a cage, and pop it into its mouth before the humans even knew it was missing. Of course, you could only do this once or twice in a given town before the humans got wise to what was happening and started taking greater precautions to protect their melons. Then you'd have to go back to goats for a while.

Most ogres stayed in the mountains and subsisted on wild animals and the occasional intrepid adventurer, but Skoorn had happened upon a caravan from which he could hear shrieks that he supposed indicated the presence of the much-coveted screech melons. He had as of this point never tasted screech melon himself, but decided it was worth the risk to see what all the fuss was about. He gradually dispatched all the humans by dropping rocks on their heads and then feasted on the three (*three!*) screech melons they had been transporting. They were sweet and juicy, and their texture was unlike anything he had experienced. After that, Skoorn knew that he couldn't go back to eating goats.

Skoorn tore up and down southern Ytrisk, plucking screech melons whenever the opportunity arose. At first it was easy: he would wait until dark, sneak into town to grab a melon or two, and then move on to the next town. But after a few towns, it seemed like the humans were on to him. They were posting guards and barring their windows; he often had to pass several towns before finding one that had any easy-to-pluck screech melons. Being a particularly clever ogre, sometimes he would backtrack and return to a town he had bypassed earlier, so that the humans could never figure out where he was headed next. Gathering the screech melons was starting to be a bit of a hassle, but Skoorn wasn't about to go back to eating those dry, crunchy goats.

After a few weeks of this, the people of southern Ytrisk were getting pretty fed up with Skoorn (although they didn't know his name). They made it clear to King Toric that if he couldn't protect them from ogres, then they would appeal to the King of Skaal. King Toric knew something had to be done.

Toric, who wasn't overly fond of his eldest son, Yoric, decided that whichever of his sons could slay the ogre would be his heir. Goric, the middle child, figured he'd wait for Yoric to be killed by the ogre and then receive the monarchy by default. Goric underestimated Yoric's cowardice, however; Yoric's only response was to attempt to assassinate Boric, the only one of Toric's sons who was actually brave and motivated enough to take on an ogre. Boric anticipated this move, escaped the assassination attempt, and made his way south to find the ogre.

Boric, who was only eighteen years old at the time, left on his horse early one morning and traveled south along the main road until nightfall, stopping at the village of Kreigsdun for the night.

Not wanting to be pestered by peasants who had some grievance against his father, he wore the uniform of the Ytriskian Messenger Corps. He traveled alone because he knew that he'd never catch the ogre if he had a whole retinue with him. The messengers were known to be surly and secretive, so it was a good cover.

As he sat in the Kreigsdun Tavern, however, he was approached by a strange man, wearing a dark cloak that concealed his features.

"Hail, Messenger," said the man. "Would you permit me to sit here with you?" His speech was colored with the aristocratic accent of the East.

Boric shrugged. "Sit if you like. I'll be off to bed soon. A messenger's day starts early."

"I won't need much time," said the man. He waved for the innkeeper to bring two mugs of beer. "My name is Brand. I hail from Avaress, on some business for the Realm. Which way are you headed?"

Boric raised an eyebrow at the man called Brand.

"Of course, of course," said Brand hurriedly, realizing his faux pas. A messenger would never reveal his destination to a stranger in a tavern. "I only asked because I meant to warn you, in case you're heading south. Things have gotten dicey down there."

"You speak of the ogre," said Boric.

The innkeeper arrived with the mugs of beer. The stranger drank, and Boric sipped slowly at his own mug, keeping an eye on the stranger.

Brand continued, "The ogre, aye. But also the townspeople. The south has lost confidence in the king. They aren't likely to welcome one of his messengers."

"I don't require a welcome," Boric said. "I will dispatch my message and be on my way."

Brand smiled. "Dispatching this particular...*message*...may be more difficult than you expect. It's a wily one, and you'll have to watch your back. And don't forget, after this message there will be others. I believe your elder brother has a message for you that remains undelivered. In fact, he may still be trying to deliver it as we speak."

Boric's hand went to his sword. "Let's drop the pretense, stranger," he said coldly. "Are you here to kill me?"

Brand laughed. "Of course not! If I were an assassin, you'd be on the back of a Wyndbahr right now, rather than enjoying a pleasant discussion of current events. I come, Boric of Ytrisk, to give you a gift."

Boric's palm remained hovering a hair's distance from the pommel of his sword. "What sort of gift?"

Brand moved his hands toward his left hip, releasing a buckle. He produced a plain-looking leather scabbard, from which protruded the hilt of a sword. He placed the sword on the table between them.

"It is called Brakslaagt," said Brand. "There are only seven of its kind. It is said that the very sight of it causes pain to ogres and others of their ilk. The slightest cut with this blade feels like the sting of a thousand scorpions to an ogre. Not only that, but it is said that the sword increases the wielder's perception of threats—that is, it allows the wielder to sense danger."

Boric snorted. "Sounds like nonsense," he said. "Wishful thinking or a sales pitch from a desperate and overly imaginative blacksmith. Keep your novelty sword. I trust my own more than I trust this one—or you, for that matter."

Brand shrugged. He finished his beer and got up from his chair. "The sword is yours," he said. "Take it or leave it. I ask nothing in return."

"I find that hard to believe," said Boric. "Clearly you want *something*."

"True," admitted the man. "What I want is for you to become King of Ytrisk." He turned to leave, taking a step toward the door. Then he turned, as if remembering something, and said, "I must warn you, though: once you pick up the sword, you may never want to let go of it."

Boric frowned. "If it's such a wonderful sword, why would I want to get rid of it?"

"That's the spirit!" said Brand, and walked out of the tavern.

# Three

Footsteps were coming up the stairs. Any second now, a gaggle of soldiers would burst from the stairwell to see Boric's corpse being dragged around the top of the tower by the hilt of his sword.

"Can I get some help here?" he cried desperately to the Eytrith.

"Alas, Boric of Ytrisk," said the Eytrith. "Thou art on thy own with this one. Thou must break this enchantment before I can transport thee to the Hall of Avandoor. I shall return in one week. Good luck!" The Eytrith slapped the neck of the Wyndbahr and it crouched and then used its powerful haunches to launch into the air. With a few flaps of its wings, they were gone.

Break the enchantment? thought Boric. How would he go about doing *that*? Perhaps by destroying his physical body? Or would that simply trap him in this form forever? His men would certainly oblige him if he gave them a chance—they would most likely burn him on a pyre right here. Would he feel the flames? And would the pyre release his spirit or imprison him on Dis for all eternity?

He decided he couldn't take the chance. Somehow he needed to find out more about this enchantment before he did anything rash—or allowed anything rash to be done to him. He needed to get his body off the tower before his men got any bright ideas. He dragged his corpse to the rear of the tower, hoisting it onto the top of the parapet. He didn't have much time to plot his next course of action, but he had a vague idea that no longer being subject to gravity he could sort of float over the edge of the parapet and lower his body to the ground. He dragged the limp corpse to the edge of the parapet and leapt from the tower. It didn't quite work out the way he planned.

His corpse slipped over the edge, jerking him downward as it fell. For a few seconds, he trailed after his own body like the tail of a kite, and then the two of them smacked into the sharply angled, rocky slope below. Spirit and flesh rolled over and over, finally coming to rest some two hundred feet farther down the slope.

Boric raised his head and was surprised to find that it was both his head—that is, the head of his disembodied spirit—and the head of the corpse. Somehow the fall had rejoined the two, so that his spirit once again occupied his body. But the body was not him—it was as if he were a ghost wearing a Boric suit. And he was certain that another jolt could just as easily knock him free of his body once again. For now, though, Boric the spirit and Boric the corpse were united in an uneasy alliance. Since he seemed to be inseparable from his body in any case, this seemed like a more sensible arrangement than dragging his corpse around as he had been.

Far above him, he heard the confused shouts of his men. They must have assumed that he had fallen and were probably looking for his body from the tower—but it was doubtful they would recognize him at this distance. It would be best for him to get out of there before they started spreading out from the tower's base to find him. He got to his feet.

He was badly injured—blood leaked from wounds on his head, his shoulder, his knees, and of course his chest, where he had been run through by that coward Randor—but he felt no pain. One of the advantages of being a wraith, he supposed. He shuddered as he noticed that he was not breathing and his heart no longer beat.

Well, he tried to shudder. He had sort of a creepy, shuddery feeling but his body didn't seem to know what to do with it. That bastard, Brand—if that was really his name—was going to answer for this. He trudged along the slope, away from the tower and toward the foothills.

As he clambered over the uneven ground, he realized that having a sword permanently attached to his hand was going to pose some practical problems. He slid the sword into the scabbard, thinking that with it at his side he would at least be less likely to accidentally stab himself. To his surprise, he found that once the sword was fully in the scabbard, he could remove his hand. Withdrawing the sword, he found that his palm was once again adhered to it. He replaced the sword once again and removed the scabbard belt, only to find that now the belt had adhered to his hand. Boric sighed and put the belt back on. One way or another, the sword was determined to stick with him.

There was only one place to go: he must find the Witch of Twyllic, who lived in a hut about a day's walk to the south. The Witch of Twyllic would know how to break the sword's spell if anyone did. Boric did his best to exorcise the thought that perhaps she wouldn't *want* to break the spell. Even the witch wasn't totally devoid of compassion, was she? And it wasn't like Boric had ever done anything to offend her *personally*. Clearly he was not to blame for her situation; she would see that, wouldn't she?

He would have to head southwest along the edge of the Dagspaal Mountains, cross a tributary of the Ytrisk River, and then continue south to the Twyllic Forest. But first he needed to get out of sight—it wouldn't do to be spotted by one of his men in this condition. Rather than taking the road south to the Brobdingdon Bridge, which joined Ytrisk and Skaal, he made his way into the foothills to the east. The way was challenging but not overly arduous, and by staying in the valleys he could avoid being seen by any sharp-eyed border sentries on either side of the river. Also, it was a relief to be facing away from the sun, which seemed to be about ten times as bright as usual. Even though the sky was mostly overcast, the glare off the rocks was nearly blinding; and whenever sunlight struck his bare skin, it burned like a branding iron. He would be greatly relieved when the sun went down.

As he headed farther toward the mountains, the river became less formidable; he knew of several places only a few hours' hike from the bridge where one could ford the stream without too much trouble. He came to the first of these just before sundown. The river was about twenty paces across here, and the water flowed over a smooth rock face in an unruffled torrent maybe a foot deep. The current moved quickly, but by walking carefully one could cross without being swept downstream. Having removed his boots, Boric took a step and was shocked at the sensation of the water on his foot. His gaping wounds still caused him no pain, but the cold water gripped his foot like a vise. He dimly recalled that wraiths were supposed to have an aversion to water, and now he knew why. Something about the touch of water on his skin brought into stark relief the unnatural contrast between his living spirit and his dead flesh. He crossed the river as quickly as he dared.

Once across, he began to head back to the southwest. The sun was setting now, and as long as he stayed well away from the bridge—which was guarded on either side by Ytriskian and Skaal soldiers—it was unlikely that he would be seen. He followed the river's edge for several miles, giving wide berth to the bridge, on which torches glowed brightly in the night. The evening air was cold, but whereas the water had given him chills, the air was oddly unaffecting. He also appeared to be immune to hunger or fatigue—his body trudged on at the goading of the spirit, heedless to its former needs. Rather than offering him comfort, however, the lack of physical cravings only served to redouble Boric's determination to rid himself of this ghoulish form as quickly as possible. Although he still retained human form at this point, he knew that his transformation to wraith was far from complete. Eventually his flesh would fall away and not long after that, any last vestige of humanity. Like most people he had never seen a wraith, but he had heard the stories. At first a wraith might try to hold on to its former life, haunting familiar venues and going through the motions of its former life, but eventually it would forget about petty human concerns—forget, in fact, that it was once human itself. Boric's greatest worry was that he would be unable to break the curse before that happened, and that he would forget that he had once dreamed of joining the other great warriors in the Hall of Avandoor. Having lost his motivation, he would wander aimlessly forever throughout the land of Dis.

Already changes were occurring within him, almost unnoticed. He realized, for instance, that he had for several hours been walking in near complete darkness without once stumbling on the uneven ground. The sun had long set but the moon had not yet arisen; by all rights he shouldn't be able to see his own feet. But another boon of his status as one of the walking dead seemed to be the ability to see almost perfectly in darkness. He could only assume this was the trade-off for his intolerance for sunlight; even now, the idea of the red-orange disk creeping over the horizon struck fear into his heart. If mere water caused him pain, what of full sunlight? He quickened his pace, determined to reach the massive sheltering oaks of the Twyllic Forest before sunrise.

Fortunately, dawn in Ytrisk was a long, gray, drawn-out affair, owing to the foreboding presence of the Dagspaal Mountains to the east. When the sky first began to lighten, Boric knew that he had another good hour before the sun would be visible. And that was propitious, for he had only just turned southward across the plain toward the forest, some five miles distant. There would be no cover between the river and the edge of the woods.

Several times he attempted to break into a run, but the jarring motion was disconcerting—he literally felt as if he was about to fall out of his own skin. As long as he moved slowly and deliberately, the body and spirit remained in sync and he still felt almost human.

The sun peeked over the zenith of the mountains while the first trees were still several hundred yards off. The glare struck his irises like twin spears. His exposed skin felt like it was on fire. Evidently he was not entirely beyond the realm of pain.

He once again began to run, realizing that the agony of full sunlight might well incapacitate him completely. He had to reach the tree line before the sun was fully above the horizon. Despite the jarring sensation, he did not pop out of his own corpse; it seemed that he was starting to get the hang of this dual existence. He shivered at the thought. Pulling his cloak tightly against him, he ran desperately to the edge of the woods.

His ordeal wasn't over when he reached the trees: the insidious rays, nearly level with the horizon, shot through the foliage, bathing the forest in swaths of glaring red. It was so bright that even through closed lids it felt like the light was drilling right through his eyes and pounding on the back of his skull. Dizzy and nauseous, feeling like his whole being was on fire, Boric stumbled blindly through the woods until he tripped over a log that reached nearly to his knees. He stayed down, pressing himself into the cool, dark cavity behind the rotting wood, waiting for the sun to climb high enough that its rays would be mostly blocked by the canopy of foliage above him.

So this is what it's like to be a wraith, he thought. Cowering behind a fallen tree, waiting for the sunrise to pass. He hadn't been this scared since he had faced the Ogre of Chathain, some twenty years earlier.

# Four

After parting ways with Brand, the mysterious stranger, Boric followed the ogre Skoorn's trail from town to town for several days, eventually ending up in a village on the border of Ytrisk and Skaal. The name of the village was Plik.

Plik was a typical border town, built on a marginally habitable plateau in the mountains between the two kingdoms. Plik's existence depended entirely on a willingness on each kingdom's part to overlook the black market trading on which its citizens subsisted. It was a place where spies, robbers, and merchants mingled freely. Justice was for sale and love could be rented by the hour.

Boric found himself in a tavern called the Velvet Gosling, nursing a beer and soaking in gossip about the ogre. Word had reached town that two infants had been plucked from their cribs the previous evening in a nearby town, and the men of the village were talking about hunting the ogre down. So far, it amounted only to talk.

"It's only a matter of time before the ogre hits Plik," said one man. "If that lazy bastard Toric isn't going to do anything about it, we need to take matters into our own hands." He downed a flagon of beer to punctuate his point. The man was built like a tree stump. Massive, blackened hands hung from arms roped with muscle, and his dirty blond hair was pulled back in a braid behind his head. A blacksmith, no doubt. And an insolent blacksmith at that, thought

Boric. A few leagues closer to Brobdingdon no one would dare refer to the king as "that lazy bastard." But things were different down here, halfway between Brobdingdon and Skaal City. Plik's allegiances swung back and forth between Skaal and Ytrisk like a sheet blowing in the wind.

"I hear the Skaal have sent an expedition into the hills to find the ogre," said another man. This one was fat, bald, and pink-cheeked and wore a finely tailored shirt and pants. A merchant of some sort.

"Ha!" bellowed the blacksmith. "Men from the same litter as those they sent against the Ytriskians at Fort Behrn last spring, no doubt. The ogre broke fast with the infants of Plik and will dine on the whelps of Skaal!"

Some disapproving mutters arose from the group. "Perhaps you should watch your tongue, Daman," said the merchant.

"An ogre plucks our children from their nurseries while they sleep and you take offense at mere talk!" spat the blacksmith.

Another man, who had been sitting alone in a corner, strode forward. He was tall and sturdily built, and wore a cloak with a hood that obscured his features.

"Seems that there is plenty of talk to be had," said the man. "What is needed is action."

"And what action do you propose, stranger?" asked the merchant.

"I propose to hunt down this ogre and kill him," said the man, flipping back his hood. He was a young man with soft features and curly blond hair. Boric thought he seemed familiar, but couldn't place him.

"And who might you be, little boy?" asked the blacksmith.

"My name is Corbet. Crown Prince of Skaal."

Could it be? thought Boric. He had met Corbet some five years earlier, when they were both just children. He remembered Corbet being something of a spoiled brat.

"My lord!" cried the men, falling to their knees. "Forgive us," said the merchant. "We didn't know it was you. We heard that the Skaal had sent men…"

"Hmph," said the prince. "A token detachment of soldiers traveling from town to town, hoping to scare the ogre back to Ytriskian territory with sheer drunken bluster. They'll never find the ogre, which is lucky for them, because the ogre would tear them to pieces. An operation like this requires some sophistication…and a knowledge of the local terrain. To your feet, gentlemen."

"I know this area like the back of my hand, m'lord!" exclaimed the merchant excitedly, as they got to their feet. Then, belatedly realizing what he was volunteering for, he added, "Perhaps I could draw you a map?"

"Nay, friend," bellowed the blacksmith, slapping the merchant on the back. "You'll be our guide. And I shall be Prince Corbet's second in command. We'll find this brute and cut out his liver, by Varnoth!" With this, he hoisted his flagon, raining beer on several nearby patrons.

"Pardon my friend," said the merchant. "He's had quite a lot to drink this evening. He doesn't know what he is saying."

"Quite all right," said the prince. "I admire his enthusiasm. You know, I had intended to hunt the ogre alone, but I do need someone who knows the area. I won't argue if you insist on accompanying me."

The merchant smiled weakly.

At this, Boric finished his beer and walked over to the men. "I will," he said.

"You'll what, Messenger?" demanded Corbet.

"Argue," said Boric. "You can't take these men into the mountains to hunt an ogre. You'll get them killed. But any fool would know that, so I can only assume you plan to use them as bait. Send your 'guides' on ahead to be devoured by the monster and then sneak up behind him with your rib-sticker there."

The merchant's pink cheeks went a few shades paler. The blacksmith seemed confused as to what was transpiring.

"I'll not brook this sort of insolence from a mere messenger!" Corbet growled, hand on the hilt of his sword. "On your knees, lad!"

"What you don't seem to realize," Boric went on, "is that while ogres can't see very well, their sense of smell is better than a hunting dog's. That ogre will smell your perfumed soaps a mile away, m'lord. Your only hope to escape is if he is overcome by nausea at your scent."

"Let's see if you can remain on your feet when your head is no longer attached to your neck!" exclaimed Corbet, making to draw his sword.

"Wait!" shouted the proprietor of the tavern, who had been watching the proceedings with detached interest. "Please, not inside!"

Corbet scowled, but said, "Outside, then, Messenger."

Boric nodded curtly and grabbed his pack from under the table where he had been sitting. He had tied the sword that Brand had given him, Brakslaagt, to the side of the pack. His own sword hung in a scabbard at his side.

He and Corbet went outside, and he gave a silver coin to a young boy in the street to watch his pack. "There'll be another for you if everything's still there when I'm done schooling this prince," Boric told the boy, who nodded and smiled at him.

The two princes drew their swords. Boric's was a simple broadsword of good quality; he had left his own sword at Kra'al Brobdingdon because with its Ytriskian markings and jewels it would have given him away as a member of the court. Corbet's sword, he noted, was a work of understated beauty—cold blue steel that almost seemed to glow in the night. There was no question: this sword was the brother of Brakslaagt.

Boric regarded the prince. Corbet was a year older than he, but his features were still slathered in a layer of baby fat. Or maybe middle age had come early for the prince. Corbet's father, King Celiac, was a giant of a man, both in height and in girth, and his offspring evinced the same tendency toward heft. Celiac was a gruff man with leathery skin that was scarred from countless battles, though; this prince's flesh was smooth and puffy. He moved nimbly enough, his sword cutting gracefully through the air as he limbered his muscles, but his poise and general affect was that of a boy prancing around the arena with a toy sword. Boric wondered if he had ever faced a real opponent. One of the hazards of being the eldest son in the royal family was that your opponents tended to let you win.

Boric did not have that problem. His older brothers, Yoric and Goric, had been beating the shit out of him for as long as he could remember—first individually and then, as Boric grew, collaboratively. Even now, both brothers were still bigger than he, but he had learned how to use their size against them. The best combat tutors were reserved for Yoric and Goric, but Boric could beat either of his brothers in a fair fight—and could even give them a run for their money in a completely unfair fight. He didn't see Corbet giving him much trouble, although it would be interesting to see how his sword performed.

The two men squared off, testing each other's defenses. Boric's sword was heavier than the one he ordinarily used, but it was a good, well-balanced blade. Boric had learned early on that in sword-fighting, there were two basic temptations: one was to let the momentum of the sword carry you around, which led to over-extending yourself and losing your balance. The other was to hold your sword close, trying to keep it completely under control as if it were a knife, which led to an overly defensive stance. The trick was to think of the sword as an extension of your arm, to find the balance between controlling the sword and letting the sword control you. Corbet clearly erred on the side of being too aggressive: he was used to opponents who paused before taking advantage of his overextension. Still, the gaps he left were small—Boric would need to time his blow just right. He sparred with Corbet for several minutes, trying to get a sense of his rhythm. Corbet was strong, too—stronger than Boric. He rained blow after blow on Boric's sword, scattering sparks and cutting notches into the blade. Corbet's own sword seemed unscathed. Boric chuckled.

Ytrisk wasn't exactly at the forefront of metallurgy but Boric knew that there were many different sorts of steel, from the malleable steel used for horseshoes and door hinges to the hard-but-brittle steel used for cooking knives. Before the rise of the Old Realm, swords had been made mostly of iron. These swords rusted easily, dulled quickly and—worst of all—were prone to bending, a trait which led to many awkward interludes in the middle of battles during which the belligerents would pause to step on their swords to straighten them out before resuming combat. The process of adding carbon to iron to make steel was for many centuries a secret of the dwarves, but when Bravnok the Great incorporated the dwarven kingdom into his empire, his smiths became privy to this knowledge. The Old Realm's smiths even improved on the dwarves' recipe, experimenting with the proportions of carbon and adding other ingredients to improve the blade's resistance to rust and its ability to hold an edge.

As with everything, though, there were trade-offs with the different sorts of steel. A sword that never dulled, for example, was bound to be brittle. Poor Corbet had probably sparred a few times with some sycophantic servant and concluded based on his sword's ability to hold an edge that it was a work of superior craftsmanship. Boric knew better.

Rather than wait for an opening, Boric decided to take advantage of Corbet's overconfidence. He let Corbet's blade bounce off his on an undercut, setting him up to take advantage of the momentum and come down hard on Boric. Boric anticipated the swing and struck back against Corbet's blade with all of his strength. Now we'll see the mettle of Corbet's steel, he thought.

Boric's blade shattered, sending fragments of steel in all directions.

The recoil of the collision had brought Corbet's sword to a halt in mid-air, a few inches from Boric's shoulder. For a moment the two men stood stunned, the shock of the impact shooting down their arms. Then Corbet smiled. Boric's sword had been reduced to a pommel and eight inches of steel. He was finished.

But Boric had one advantage: an eight-inch blade is lighter and faster than a three-foot blade. Boric hurled the remnant of his sword at Corbet's face, hilt first. The pommel struck Corbet in the forehead, knocking his head back. Boric bent his knees and kicked, throwing his body backward as Corbet swung wildly, his blade scribing a red line across Boric's cheek. Boric turned sideways, maintaining his momentum by rolling on his side away from Corbet. Being on the ground was a tactical disadvantage, but it was the only way to get out of the range of Corbet's sword.

He got to his knees and scrambled away from the sound of Corbet's advancing footsteps. This was not going as well as he had hoped.

"You fight well for a messenger, boy," said Corbet snidely. "It will be a shame to cut your throat."

Boric turned to face Corbet, who had stopped advancing to gloat. Boric got to his feet. He could at least die with some dignity. Corbet would probably spare his life if he revealed his identity, but Boric was too proud to do that. Better to die as a messenger than to save his skin by confessing to his charade. Corbet brought his sword back, poised to strike.

"Sir," said a small voice to Boric's left. Boric turned to see the boy he had entrusted with his possessions running toward him. The boy was holding, on his outstretched palms, a sword in a scabbard. *Brakslaagt*.

"Wait!" shouted Boric. Corbet had already begun his stroke. The boy was running right into the path of its arc.

The boy stopped in front of Boric, offering him the sword. Boric grabbed the hilt of Brakslaagt with his right hand and the top of the scabbard with his left, thrusting his upper torso forward and his arms apart. His left arm sent the boy flying into crowd and his right arm brought the sword up to meet Corbet's. The sound of the blades clashing was like hailstones on a tin roof. Boric straightened and took a step back.

The two men regarded each other for a moment.

"Nice sword," said Corbet. He was trying to sound jovial but there was an undercurrent of worry in his voice.

Boric sliced the blade through the air several times. It was surprisingly light, considering its strength and durability—assuming it was made of the same material as Corbet's sword. Whatever the weakness of this steel was, it hadn't yet revealed itself.

"Thanks," he said. "It was a gift." Boric thrust at Corbet's midsection and Corbet knocked the blade to the side, answering with a sweep at Boric's neck. Boric parried and followed with a swift chop at Corbet's left side, which Corbet dodged.

Boric had to admit Brakslaagt felt good in his hand. It was light for its size, but well-balanced and substantial. Sharp, too— the edge of the blade gleamed as if it has just been honed. One good slice with that blade and the slicee would be dead. And Corbet's sword appeared to be its equal. It was time to end this before someone got hurt.

Corbet jabbed at Boric's groin and Boric parried and sliced at Corbet's neck. Corbet ducked and sliced at Boric's legs. Boric parried.

The two men sparred for another minute, Boric's swings gradually becoming more desultory, giving Corbet the impression that he was tiring. Corbet took advantage of his sluggishness, becoming bolder in his attacks. Finally the moment came that Boric was waiting for: Corbet lunged, overextending himself and exposing his flank. Boric dodged and brought his Brakslaagt down on Corbet's skull, the flat of the blade striking him with a sickening *thump*. Corbet's eyes rolled upward and he fell limp to the ground.

Boric walked to the boy guarding his pack. The boy was staring open-mouthed at Corbet.

"Is he dead?"

"Nah," said Boric. "Just sleeping." He handed the boy a silver coin. "Thanks for your help. See that the innkeeper takes care of the prince."

The boy nodded eagerly. He had probably never held a coin made from real silver before that night—let alone two of them.

"Now," said Boric, "who wants to kill an ogre?"

# Five

Boric had been trudging along the dark forest path for hours when he came upon a clearing, in the middle of which was a small cottage, the home of the Witch of Twyllic. He regarded the cottage with some trepidation. There weren't many people Boric the Implacable was afraid of. None, in fact, other than the Witch of Twyllic. But he had no choice: the witch was the only one who might be able to tell him how to break his curse.

Before he could talk to the witch, however, he had to cross the clearing, which meant traversing a good twenty paces of open ground in broad daylight. His eyes hurt just looking at the sunlight reflecting off the cottage's thatched roof. He could wait until dark, but he didn't want to spend any longer as a wraith than he absolutely had to. He was already growing accustomed to being a spirit occupying a corpse; soon he feared that he would forget altogether what it was like to be human.

Boric retreated a ways into the forest and took a seat on a moss-covered log. He removed his armor and clothing and inspected his body. The wounds were still there, but they had stopped bleeding and caused him no pain. Even sticking his fingers into the gaping wound in his chest evoked only a sort of dull ache, as if someone was gently pressing the end of a walking stick into his ribs. He shuddered at the sensation.

His flesh was pale and had begun to sag appallingly. Soon he would begin to rot. Something needed to be done before that happened. He stood up and started to get dressed.

Behind him, a twig snapped. Boric sprang for his sword and spun around. Before him stood a small figure wearing a dingy gray robe and a wide-brimmed hat. The Witch of Twyllic. Forty years earlier she might have been reasonably attractive, but half a lifetime in the forest had taken its toll. Her dishwater-gray hair was thin and ratty and her face looked like a piece of paper that had been wadded up and retrieved from the trash.

"What are you doing out here?" she snapped, in a surprisingly shrill tone.

"I, uh…" Boric started. He realized that his voice had turned into a dry rasp.

"I got enough problems without half-naked wraiths lurking about," said the witch. "What's your business here, wraith?"

"Well," said Boric, "I was hoping you could help me. You see, I've been cursed."

"You don't say!" exclaimed the witch. "So was I! Tell me, wraith, were you thrown out of the court of Kra'al Brobdingdon on trumped-up charges of practicing black magic and forced into thirty-eight years of exile?"

"Well, no," said Boric. "But I was recently killed and by all rights should be drinking mead in the Halls of Avandoor. Instead, as you see, I am occupying my own corpse."

"We've all got problems," said the witch with a shrug.

"Please," said Boric. "All I want is to die a natural death before I become even more of a monster. Your knowledge of the dark arts is well known throughout Ytrisk—"

"Bah!" growled the witch. "Cease your foolish talk and I will do what I can for you. Follow me."

The witch strode past him toward the cottage.

"I...ah..." said Boric.

"Afraid of a little sunlight, are you?" asked the witch, turning back to face him. "Part of the price of your bargain, I suppose. Well, you know where to find me." She walked across the clearing and disappeared into the cottage.

Boric cursed and squinted up at the dazzling bright blue sky. Ytrisk was known for its almost invariably gray and depressing weather, but today there was hardly a cloud in the sky. He waited nearly an hour for a little puffy cloud to pass in front of the sun before sprinting across the clearing, his cloak wrapped tightly about him. The sunlight burned even through the thick cloak.

Unable to see where he was going, he slammed abruptly into the door of the cottage. "Open up!" he cried. His upper back and face felt like they were on fire.

"Who is it?" called the witch voice from inside.

"Boric!" rasped Boric.

"Boric who?"

"Boric the wraith! Please, it burns!"

The door opened and the witch regarded him suspiciously. "I don't get it," she said.

Boric rushed past her and fell to the floor, shaking feverishly.

The witch shrugged and closed the door, returning to a pot of stew she was cooking. The scent was nauseating.

"Ugh," Boric groaned, still writhing on the floor. "What *is* that?"

"Rabbit," said the witch. "You want some?"

If Boric had been capable of vomiting, he would have.

"Oh, I forgot!" exclaimed the witch. "You're undead. The smell of cooking meat probably nauseates you!"

Boric grunted and nodded his head weakly.

"Pity," she said. She put a lid on the pot and opened the shuttered windows. The light hurt Boric's eyes, but it was preferable to the stench of the stew. After some time, he shakily got to his feet and took a seat in a nearby chair.

"Now, what seems to be the problem?" asked the witch.

Boric was beginning to lose patience. "I'm a *corpse*," he snarled.

"Well, sure," agreed the witch, "but plenty of corpses get on just fine. Perhaps your problem is that your expectations are too high. Try lying down for a bit."

"Damn it, woman!" growled Boric. "I won't be spoken to in this matter. Do you know who I am?"

"I know who you *were*," laughed the witch. "Boric the Implacable, King of Ytrisk. Who you *are* is another matter. Or should I say, *what* you are. You're a sack of rotting meat, Boric the Impractical."

"I came here for your help, witch," rasped Boric, "not to be insulted."

"You came here because although I am an embarrassment to the court of Ytrisk, I remain the only one in the kingdom who knows anything of the arcane arts. You cast me out and then go looking for me amongst the trash. I insult you because you're a fool, Boric the Impractical, just like your mother and father were."

Boric had seen this coming. Best to get it over with.

The Witch of Twyllic hadn't always lived alone in a cottage in the woods. She was born the daughter of one of the Librarians of Avaress, in the final days of the Old Realm. Her parents were killed when Avaress was overrun by barbarians and the library was destroyed, and she escaped from the capital to Ytrisk with a merchant caravan, offering her services as a bookkeeper in exchange for safe passage out of the capital. Even at the height of the Old Realm, literacy and knowledge of basic mathematics were rare among commoners. Besides, she took up little space and didn't eat much. She was only ten years old.

Before she was the Witch of Twyllic, her name was Anna. Anna was essentially a slave to a merchant for two years, but her employer eventually fell afoul of Ytriskian law, and his assets—including Anna—were confiscated. She was put to work as a midwife's assistant. She had an astonishing memory and had spent most of her childhood devouring the books of the great Library of Avaress; she could recall details from hundreds of the books on subjects from agriculture and anatomy to history and religion. On more than one occasion, she shamed the king's advisors with her superior knowledge on some obscure matter. But being female, the greatest position she could aspire to in the court was that of head midwife.

Sometime after she had reached that exalted position, and after eight years of faithful service to the court, she was accused of witchcraft and exiled to the periphery of the kingdom. Witchcraft was one of those obscure crimes that was seen so seldom that court officials worried constantly that they weren't looking hard enough. If it weren't for the occasional appearance of someone who clearly fit the definition, no one would even know what a witch looked like.

The exercise of magic was not technically illegal in Ytrisk; the court occasionally employed diviners and sorcerers for a variety of purposes. It was only dark magic that was met with disapproval. Dark magic was also ill-defined, but in general it seemed to possess at least two of these three characteristics:

1. It didn't work or had undesirable side effects.
2. It embarrassed someone in power.
3. It was practiced by one's enemies or a woman.

Boric, not being a complete idiot, was well aware of the conveniently flexible definition of "dark magic" used by the court, but Anna's exile had occurred before he was born, and when he ascended to the throne he had bigger things to worry about than the justness of a sentence carried out a quarter of a century earlier.

In any case, Boric had figured, the woman should be grateful she was allowed to live. Most witches were executed in a carefully prescribed and logistically complex series of tortures that culminated in the witch being drowned while on fire.

"I am sorry for your misfortune," said Boric, "but as you know, the sentence for witchcraft is death. My father showed you considerable mercy in—"

"Your father tossed me out like garbage!" spat the witch. "One more word of Toric's mercy and I'll pour rabbit stew on your head!"

"Please," Boric tried again. "I am sorry for any mistreatment you suffered at the hand of my father."

"You were king for thirteen years, Boric. You could have ended my exile at any time."

"It is true," Boric admitted. "However, I was not privy to the details of your case—"

"Nor did you make any effort to familiarize yourself with them. In life, you didn't give me a second thought. But now that you're dead, you come running to me."

"Again, I apologize—"

"Cease your wheedling!" the witch spat. "What is it that you expect me to do for you?"

"I was hoping you could undo my curse. Allow me to die in peace, so that my spirit can rest in the Hall of Avandoor."

"Your curse!" hissed the witch. "A curse is something forced upon you, like being exiled in the woods for imagined crimes. What you are experiencing is the downside of a bargain that you entered into with your eyes wide open. What did you think was going to happen when you accepted an enchanted blade from a mysterious stranger? Does that sound like the sort of thing that would have a happy ending?"

Boric was speechless for a moment. "You know of my meeting with Brand?"

"I know that he gave six enchanted blades to kings or princes of the Six Kingdoms, one per kingdom. And I know the bargain that goes with the blades. First the blade serves you, then you serve the blade."

"I guess I figured the bargain ended when I died."

"You figured wrong."

"Is there anything you can do about it?"

The witch shook her head grimly. "No one knows how to break the curse of the Blades of Brakboorn. I suspect the answer lies with the seventh blade, Orthslaagt, the one that Brand holds."

"Then I shall hunt down Brand and take Orthslaagt from him—along with his right arm, if I have to!"

"Fool!" spat the witch. "That is exactly what Brand hopes you will do. You are being pulled toward him by the inexorable magic of the blade. Your humanity is slipping away, Boric, your own volition being replaced by the will of Lord Brand."

"Lord Brand!" exclaimed Boric. "He has pretensions to nobility, does he?"

"He has pretension to more than that, I understand. Occasionally I receive visitors from the east seeking my expertise. One benefit of being officially exiled for witchcraft, you know, is that you get a reputation abroad. Recently news has reached me that Brand is assembling a new kingdom in the east. He rules a petty fiefdom beyond the Wastes of Preel. Some even say he plans to unify all the territory of the Old Realm under his rule."

"Ridiculous!" Boric rasped. "The Six Kingdoms have grown fiercely independent since the Fall."

"And they are constantly fighting amongst themselves," added the witch. "A bold man might see an opportunity in the current situation."

"All the more reason for me to hunt down Brand and kill him," said Boric. "He isn't to be trusted with that sort of power."

"If you go to him, you will fall under his power," repeated the witch. "Don't say I didn't warn you."

"Then what would you have me do, witch?" Boric demanded. "Run from him until I'm a heap of dry bones?"

"Consider it a tactical retreat," advised the witch. "You must fight the pull of Orthslaagt until you are strong enough to deal with Brand on your own terms."

"Strong enough!" growled Brand. "My flesh is rotting away as we speak! My humanity is draining away, and I am becoming a monster! I must seek out Brand now, while I still remember what it was to be human!"

"No!" cried the witch. "You must accept that you are no longer human. You must give up your former ways of thinking and embrace your status as undead. Brand's power over you arises from your desire to regain your humanity. When you let that go, Brand will no longer be able to control you."

"I don't want to regain my humanity!" Boric protested. "I simply want to *die*."

The witch laughed. "Yes, but you want to die as a *human being*. You want to go straight from your heroic life to a jubilant afterlife, without this pesky detour into the gray wasteland of undeath. You must accept that you are a wraith, a foul creature of the night, hated by the living. When you have done that, you will be free to kill Brand and take Orthslaagt from him."

"But when I have become fully a wraith, I will no longer want to be free of Orthslaagt!"

"A paradox, one must admit," said the witch, nodding. "Sadly, that is the only answer. There is one thing I can do for you, though."

"Please," said Boric. "Whatever you can do, I will be forever grateful."

"You should be a bit more hesitant about making eternal commitments," the witch scolded. "Take your clothes off."

The one thing that the witch could do for Boric turned out to be embalming him, wrapping him with cloth saturated in foul-smelling substances that promised to slow the process of decay. The wrappings were tight but oddly comforting; they made Boric feel less like he was going to fall apart at any moment. She left only his eyes uncovered; at first he had objected to having his mouth and nose wrapped but she pointed out that he no longer needed to either eat or breathe—and that unless it was secured, his jaw would probably eventually fall off. He wasn't sure he actually needed his jaw to speak; his voice seemed to emit from his mouth in some ghostly fashion, utilizing neither the flow of air across his vocal cords nor the movement of his lips and tongue (although he continued to move these muscles, like a puppet mimicking the speech of the puppeteer). Still, losing his jaw would make him look even more monstrous, and it was important that he at least appear human for as long as possible. When he put on his clothing and armor and covered his head with his cloak, he looked almost normal. She had also painted over the markings on his armor with pitch, both so that he'd be less visible in the dark ("a wraith has to be able to skulk") and so that he wouldn't be recognized as the former King of Ytrisk.

By the time she had finished, it was nearly dark outside. The witch lit a lamp and stood back, regarding her work with what Boric could only imagine was pride. She seemed on the verge of saying something when the door to the cottage flew open and three dark figures entered the room, their footsteps eerily quiet. They wore dark cloaks and black leather gloves, their eyes pinpoints of red light burning like coals in faces wrapped in black cloth. Each of them carried a broadsword that was an exact likeness of Brakslaagt.

"Boric the Implacable, son of Toric," hissed the figure at the lead of the group. "Our master has summoned you."

# Six

After his decisive victory over the Crown Prince of Skaal, Boric had no trouble enlisting locals to assist him in his efforts to vanquish the ogre. The only local whose help Boric really wanted was the chubby, bald-headed merchant, but he let the blacksmith come along because he wasn't sure the merchant would go along with what he was planning without some prodding from his friend.

"Where are we going?" asked the merchant, whose name was Padmos, as he and the blacksmith tailed Boric through the village. "Surely you don't mean to hunt the ogre at night."

"On my way here I rode past an abandoned house on the edge of town," said Boric. "That's where we're going to wait for the ogre." Boric carried ahead of him a small lantern, allowing them to make their way through the darkened streets.

"That's the old miller's house," said the blacksmith, whose name was Daman. "It's completely burned out. The roof is falling in."

"The ogre isn't going to concern himself with the structural integrity of the house," replied Boric. "Careful with that thing." This last was directed at Daman, who was swinging a sword through the air in lazy arcs. He had insisted on stopping by his shop and picking up the sword, which he had made on a slow day a few weeks earlier. Like Daman himself, the sword was crude but functional. Boric didn't really like the idea of the big oaf carrying a sword, but he didn't want to waste time arguing. For his part, Boric had decided to hold on to Brakslaagt.

Daman and Padmos, the merchant, muttered back and forth behind Boric. While they were relieved not to be heading out into the hills at night to hunt the ogre, they weren't so sure about spending the night in a burned-out house on the edge of town. What made this messenger think that the ogre would be coming here? And why did a messenger care so much about a rogue ogre anyway? Didn't he have messages to deliver?

Boric led the two men to the old house. It hadn't been much of a house even before it had burned, and now it was just a blackened husk of its former self. Boric led the men into the house, which was really just a one-room cottage with a dirt floor. He set the lantern on the floor and pulled a rolled-up sheet of parchment from his pack, spreading it out on the ground. It was a map of Ytrisk and the northern part of Skaal. The map was old and faded, but along the main north-south road through Ytrisk were a number of darker characters that seemed to have been added recently.

Daman, who had probably never seen a map before, frowned at the strange drawing, but Padmos the merchant seemed to understand what it was. "What are these markings?" he asked.

"Numbers," said Boric. "You're familiar with Avaressian numerals?"

The merchant nodded.

"The numbers indicate the order of the ogre's attacks. Number one, here, represents the first attack."

"Some numbers are missing," observed the merchant.

"The ogre doesn't attack every day. He takes every third day off. You see? One, two, four, five, seven, eight, ten, eleven. The multiples of three are missing."

"A pattern!" exclaimed the merchant excitedly.

"Indeed," replied Boric. "And that's not all. As you know, most of the towns in southern Ytrisk are located at sites of former outposts of the Old Realm, every three miles, give or take. Notice anything about the spacing of the attacks?"

The merchant studied the map. After a moment, his eyes lit up. "He attacks, travels three towns north, then travels four towns south and attacks again. The gap in the attacks occurs when he is traveling the extra distance. But that means that the next town to be attacked is Plik!"

"Correct," said Boric. "He's due to attack here tonight, if the pattern holds."

"But why would the ogre travel in such a predictable way?" asked Padmos.

Boric shrugged. "I doubt he's aware of the pattern. Ogres are stupid. This one seems to be just smart enough to avoid attacking town after town in direct succession, but not smart enough to be truly random about it. Still, it took me a while to figure out the pattern. After the attack in Sorvekt two nights ago, I realized he would be coming here next. Which is why I'm here."

"Why *are* you here?" asked Daman suspiciously. "What concern of yours is this ogre?"

Boric realized he was going to have to level with his compatriots. After tonight, with any luck, he wouldn't need to keep his identity secret anyway. Once the ogre was dispatched, he could return to Kra'al Brobdingdon victorious.

"I'm not a messenger," said Boric. "My name is Boric, son of Toric, King of Ytrisk."

"M'lord!" exclaimed both men, falling to their knees.

"All right, enough of that," said Boric. "We have an ogre to kill."

The men got to their feet, brushing charcoal from their knees. "If I may ask, m'lord, why did you come here in disguise?"

"Killing an ogre requires some discretion and stealth," said Boric. "Ogres are powerful and cruel, but also craven. They spook easily. Fortunately I was able to head off brave Prince Corbet before he stank up the hills with the stench of lavender and rose petals. Now, you two find some wood and help me build a fire."

"A fire?" asked Daman. "Is that a good idea? We might attract the ogre."

"Well, what did you think we were trying to do?" asked Boric.

The blacksmith nodded slowly, the reality of the situation dawning on him. The two men went out to find firewood.

"Make as much noise as you can!" called Boric after them.

"I thought we didn't want to spook the ogre?" said Padmos, ducking his head back inside.

"Oh, he's not going to feel threatened by a couple of idiots stomping about in the dark," said Boric. After a moment he added, thoughtfully, "No offense."

Daman grumbled something and the two left again. After a few minutes, they returned, each bearing an armload of twigs and wood scraps. Daman assembled a mass of kindling and straw and expertly got a flame going with a piece of flint and a small steel bar. It wasn't long before the fire was burning brightly in the center of the room, warming them nicely against the cool air wafting in through the gaping windows.

"Don't get too comfortable," said Boric. "The light should draw the ogre's attention, but now we need some bait."

"Bait?" asked Padmos, scratching his gleaming pink scalp. "The ogre eats babies. We can't leave an infant out for the ogre!"

"No, we can't," agreed Boric. "But we've got something almost as good."

Surprisingly, Daman caught his implication before Padmos did. The burly blacksmith broke into hearty laughter.

"What?" asked the merchant angrily. "What am I missing?" His soft white cheeks reddened as he spoke, causing Daman to tumble to the ground, clutching his sides. Tears rolled down the blacksmith's face.

"Oh, no!" exclaimed the merchant, as a realization washed over him. "You are *not* using me as bait!"

"Come on, Padmos," cried Daman, still lying on the ground. "You'll be a hero!"

"Bah!" grumbled the merchant, rubbing his fleshy bald pate.

"He's right," said Boric. "I'll be heading back to Brobdingdon as soon as we're done, so you two can take all the credit for slaying the ogre. Plus, there's a gold in it for each of you."

Daman was suitably impressed with this but Padmos still looked unconvinced. "Two gold," he said. "You gave that kid at the tavern two silver just for watching your pack."

"That kid saved my life," Boric said. "Fine. Two gold for each of you. One now, one when the ogre's dead. Fair?"

The two men grunted assent and Boric handed each of them a gold coin.

"Now, Padmos," said Boric. "Let me see that lustrous noggin of yours."

Padmos stepped forward uncertainly, leaning his head toward Boric.

"Excellent," exclaimed Boric. He uncorked a small bottle and poured a bit of liquid onto Padmos's head, smearing it around with his other hand.

"Augh!" Padmos cried. "What is that?"

"Sour milk," answered Boric. "We want you to smell like a baby, after all. Let's get some on your tunic."

"No, sir!" said Padmos. "M'lord, I'm all for catching this ogre, but I won't be humiliated in this manner!"

"Really?" asked Boric. "How would you like to be humiliated? I have another bottle, if you really want to go for authenticity."

"What's in the other bottle?" asked Padmos skeptically.

"Well, it's not milk, I'll tell you that."

Padmos reluctantly agreed to be doused with the sour milk.

"There! Now you smell like a baby!" exclaimed Boric. "All right, let's hear you cry."

"Cry?" said the merchant dubiously.

"Babies cry," said Boric. "Surely you've heard one."

"Some babies are sound sleepers," offered Padmos weakly. "Some babies hardly make a peep."

"Not the ones who get eaten by ogres," chided Boric. "Come on, now."

Padmos gave a little bleat.

"What are you, a sheep?" asked Boric. "Cry like you mean it!"

Padmos bleated a bit louder.

"Wow, you are a terrible baby," observed Boric. "If you were my baby, I'd be praying that an ogre would eat you."

"I'm doing my best!" protested the merchant. "I'd like to see you do better!"

Boric let loose an impassioned cry, startling Padmos.

"Not bad," admitted the merchant.

"No, no," said Daman. "It's like this." The blacksmith broke into a heartrending wail.

"Brilliant!" exclaimed Boric. "All right, Daman, you're on sound effects."

"I what?" asked Daman. "No, I was just demonstrating—"

"And a fine demonstration it was," said Boric. "Now you just need to do it for the ogre." He ushered the two over to the eastern window, the direction he expected the ogre to be coming from. He had Padmos crouch on the ground under the window, so that his bald head was just visible from outside. He stationed Daman next to Padmos, coaching the big man to wail as loudly as he could.

"Wonderful!" exclaimed Boric over Daman's incessant bleating. "Together you two make a formidable infant." Boric turned to leave.

"Wait!" cried Padmos. "Where are you going?"

"Outside," said Boric. "I can't take the racket in here. And it stinks like sour milk."

# Seven

Boric drew Brakslaagt and faced the three intruders. The witch gasped and shrank back.

"It is pointless to fight us, brother," hissed the wraith in front. "You are one of us, Slaagtghast."

"Back off!" shouted Boric in what he intended to be a growl but ended up sounding distressingly similar to the hiss of the wraith. "I'll deal with Brand in my own time!"

The wraiths moved closer. "Our lord has summoned you, Slaagtghast. You cannot refuse his call." Something in the lead wraith's aspect seemed oddly familiar to Boric.

"Why do you keep calling me that?" Boric demanded angrily. "I'm Boric, son of Toric, King of Ytrisk!"

A rustling sound like the raking of leaves arose from the macabre trio. Boric realized they were laughing at him. "We dead cannot be kings," rasped the leader. "We dead have no fathers. We have only our Master and the brethren of the Brakboorn. You are Slaagtghast, holder of Brakslaagt."

Boric realized now why the leader seemed familiar. He had faced this man before.

"Corbet?" he gasped.

The leader hissed fiercely. "Corbet is dead!" he shrieked. "I am Vektghast, servant of Lord Brand!" He raised his sword while the other two wraiths moved to flank Boric.

Boric hesitated, unsure what to do. Could the wraiths kill him? That is, release his spirit from his corpse? He doubted it. Probably they would just hack his body to pieces, removing that much more of his humanity. Corbet and the other wraiths seemed to be mostly an assemblage of torn clothes, chainmail, and steel plates; he wasn't sure there was any flesh left beneath their vaguely insect-like carapaces. Corbet, he knew, had been dead for some seven years. And seven years from now, thought Boric, that will be me.

He let his sword fall to his side. This was not a battle he could win. If neither he nor his opponents could be killed, then this encounter could only end with him fleeing or surrendering. Best to go along with the wraiths until an opportunity to escape presented itself.

"I see you have recognized the futility of resistance," the wraith that was Corbet said. "It is for the best. I resisted too at first, and lost my head as a result."

Boric saw that indeed Corbet's helm appeared to be empty except for two pinpoints of red light. That's what being headstrong got you apparently. Boric slid Brakslaagt into its scabbard and held out his arms in a gesture of surrender.

As the wraiths converged on him, Boric felt something like a red-hot blade being pressed against his neck. He gasped in pain as a mass of brown goo flew past him, striking the three wraiths square in what remained of their faces. "Gaaahhh!" they cried. "What sorcery is this?"

"Rabbit stew," said the witch. "Run, Boric!"

Boric darted past the wraiths, who were hissing and scream-ing at the foul liquid steaming inside their helms. Boric, himself nearly overcome with nausea at the stench, ran outside into the dark and did his best to scrape the remnants of stew off his neck and shoulders. He felt instantly refreshed and invigorated in the cold night air.

He saw three horses tied to trees near the edge of the clearing and ran toward them. The beasts whinnied nervously as he approached; clearly they had no love for the undead. Slicing through their reins with Brakslaagt, he proceeded to slap two of the horses on their hindquarters with the flat of the blade, spooking them to dart into the forest. He leapt onto the third horse and kicked his heels into its sides. "Hyah!"

The three wraiths stumbled out of the witch's cottage, cursing and hissing. "After him!" shrieked the one who had been Corbet.

The horse darted past the wraiths and onto the trail. It seemed hesitant to reenter the woods, but Boric urged it on mercilessly. As the horse galloped down the trail, Boric spared a glance behind him. The three wraiths were following closely but couldn't keep pace with the horse and rapidly fell behind. Then, just when Boric was starting to think he was safe, the horse collapsed beneath him, as if one of its front legs had given way. Boric flew over the horse's head, spinning head over heels, and landed flat on his back some ten paces down the trail.

"Accursed beast!" spat Boric, looking back at the horse. "What do you think you're…" But then Boric saw that the animal was lying on the ground, shuddering and nuzzling its foreleg, which was bent at an unnatural angle. It had tripped over a root protruding from the ground.

"Idiot!" muttered Boric, this time at himself. The horse hadn't been able to see the root in the near total darkness of the forest path. He had forgotten that living creatures—even horses—needed light to see. No wonder the poor animal had hesitated.

Boric got up and ran, with the three wraiths not far behind. Even with his preternatural night vision, running down a narrow, ill-maintained trail through the Forest of Twyllic was a hazardous occupation. The ground was uneven and littered with rocks, dead branches, and roots, and he frequently had to dodge low-hanging branches. If he fell or got caught on a branch, the game was up: the wraiths would be upon him. And then…what? They'd haul him in front of Lord Brand, presumably. Boric realized as he thought this that there was nothing he wanted more than to face his tormentor. Maybe the witch was wrong, and that if Boric went to Brand now, while he still possessed his wits, he could strike him down, freeing himself and the other wraiths from his control. Still, it galled him that Brand thought he could send the other wraiths to fetch him as if he were Brand's property. No, as much as he wanted to face Brand, he would do it on his own terms.

Distracted by his thoughts, Boric suddenly realized he had left the trail. Before he could stop running, he lost his footing and found himself tumbling uncontrollably down a steep embankment, thrashing through shrubs and saplings on the way down. Finally he smacked into the trunk of a tree and came to a stop, dazed. Far above, he heard movement and harsh whispers. Had the other wraiths seen him fall? He remained as still as he could—helped in this endeavor by having neither breath nor a heartbeat—and hoped the wraiths were continuing on the path above. After a moment, the sounds faded into the distance.

Boric got to his feet, carefully moving down the slope. It wouldn't be long before the wraiths realized their mistake and came back for him. Working his way from shrub to shrub, he eventually made it to the bottom, which was a dry creek bed about fifty feet across. It was overrun by trees and bushes, but it looked to be traversable with some effort. Considering his options for a moment—left would take him roughly north, toward the witch's cottage, and right would take him farther south, the direction he had been going—he decided to continue south. This was the direction the wraiths would expect him to take, but he didn't dare head back into Ytriskian territory. He was too likely to be recognized by his fellow countrymen, who harbored a long-standing superstition regarding walking corpses. Anywhere else, he might pass as a wounded soldier wrapped in bandages—as long as he wasn't inspected too closely.

He trudged along the creek bed for several hours, using Brakslaagt as a machete to hack through the brush. When he came to a more gently sloping section of the ravine, he climbed back up and found his way to the path. Stopping for a moment to listen, he heard no sounds in either direction other than the hooting of owls and rustling of the wind through the trees. There was no way to know whether the wraiths were ahead of him or behind him, or what direction they were going—or whether they had split up to cover more ground. His best bet was to continue southward and keep an eye out for them.

He trudged glumly through the forest all night and the next day. In most places the forest provided enough cover that the sunlight wasn't overly bothersome, but occasionally he had to hack through the underbrush to avoid patches of full daylight. Eventually the sun set again, and Boric kept moving roughly south. In the midafternoon of the third day since he entered the forest, he came to the southern edge, where the trees gave way to the sandy hills to the northeast of the Kingdom of Skaal. This land was largely unpopulated, being too uneven and infertile to be used as cropland and too distant from trading routes to sustain a settlement. The only people Boric would run into here would be bandits and other unsavory folk—not that Boric the wraith had any reason to fear such people. His primary fear remained the merciless sunlight that assaulted the scrubby hillsides.

Boric found a fallen tree some distance from the trail, a hundred yards or so from where the trees began to thin. Being incapable of sleep, he would have to wait here until dark. Up till now Boric had given little thought to his next move; he was concerned mainly with putting as much distance as possible between him and the other wraiths. The trail had forked several times and each time Boric had stayed to the left, working his way farther from the Kingdom of Ytrisk. He supposed that the wraiths, if they were trying to anticipate his moves, would assume that he would stay close to more familiar and hospitable lands. But as much as Boric wished to retain his humanity, he had accepted that the comfort of the familiar was a dangerous temptation and that what was once hospitable was now hostile. To survive, he had to think like a wraith. His allies now were darkness, cold, and solitude.

But allies to what end? How would he ever address Brand's claim on him if he remained hiding out in the wilderness, slowly becoming an ever-paler copy of the once renowned King Boric? Isolation from human society would only accelerate the process of him devolving into a baleful creature of darkness. Was that really what the witch was suggesting? That he should intentionally become a monster? Or could he somehow come to terms with his wraithness without becoming an abomination? It seemed impossible. The very existence of the undead was a violation of the natural order of things.

When the sun had once again set, he continued southward, eventually coming to the great east-west road that connected Avaress with the western kingdoms. He now had a choice to make: he could turn west and head toward Skaal—this had the advantage of being the least expected course of action, but the disadvantage of being suicidal: the only thing hated more in Skaal than a Ytriskian king was an undead Ytriskian king. To the east lay Avaressa, the capital of Avaress and once-center of the Old Realm. He'd be less likely to be recognized in Avaressa, and the Avaressian merchants might know something about the machinations of the mysterious Brand. It would be difficult to inquire of anyone directly, but perhaps he could hide in the corner of a tavern and overhear some talk. If Brand really were planning a new empire, then surely there would be some rumors flying around in the taverns of Avaressa. Boric turned east.

It had been many years since Boric had traveled this way, and he had only a vague recollection of the geography of the area. In particular, he couldn't recall whether there were any dense woods or caves nearby. The last time he had been down this road he hadn't been particularly concerned with identifying places where a wraith could safely wait out the daylight. He grew more anxious as the night wore on and the landscape remained hilly but otherwise featureless. The sparse, scrubby trees would provide no shade.

Less than an hour before dawn he came upon a barely perceptible path leading southward. In fact, even when he stood and studied the ground, Boric couldn't be entirely certain that it *was* a path. There was nothing particularly path-like that he could point to; there were no markers of any kind and although the ground was flat and the grass was sparse, there was no perceivable linear shape to it. What he experienced was more of a vague intuition that living creatures occasionally passed here. Did he now possess a heightened sensitivity to life just as he had for sunlight? Whatever it was, he was virtually certain that he could have walked past this place a hundred times in full daylight as a mortal man and noticed nothing whatsoever.

If it was a path, he thought, then perhaps it led to some forgotten settlement, a town that had been abandoned after the fall of the Old Realm. That meant the possibility of finding a structure in which he could hide. As there was nothing remotely promising in any other direction, he made his way south, following his sense of the path as best he could.

# Eight

As serious as his situation was, Boric found it difficult not to laugh at the sight of Padmos's bald pate reflecting the bluish moonlight through the window of the old burned-out house. The uncanny infantile wails of Daman the blacksmith emitting from somewhere inside didn't help his composure either.

Boric was perched uncomfortably on a bough of a nearby oak tree, about twelve feet up and a hundred feet downwind from the miller's house. As long as the ogre didn't approach from behind him, he had a good chance of remaining unnoticed while the ogre was distracted by the bait. And if the ogre did approach from behind? Well, ogres weren't known for their tree-climbing abilities, were they? Boric wracked his memory, trying to recall a story in which an ogre climbed a tree. He came up with nothing, but then neither could he recall a story in which an ogre had been drawn into the open by a bald merchant doused with sour milk and a mewling blacksmith. Sometimes stories weren't much help.

"Prince Boric!" called a voice from the house. It was Padmos. "How much longer?"

Boric gritted his teeth but didn't reply. Hadn't he warned those two about breaking character? If they spooked the ogre, he'd have to travel to the next town—assuming they didn't cause the ogre to alter his pattern—and do this all over again. Meanwhile, Boric's idiot brothers were undoubtedly scheming against him back at Kra'al Brobdingdon, trying to figure out how they were going to cheat him out of his spoils if he defeated the ogre. He needed to get this over with and get back home as quickly as possible.

"Prince Boric!" called Padmos again. "I don't think this is working!"

"Quiet, you moron!" hissed Daman, momentarily ceasing his wailing.

"I think he's left us," said Padmos. "Left us alone to be ripped apart by an ogre. Figures!"

"Waaaaahhhhh!" cried Daman, doing his best to drown out Padmos's mutterings.

"Stop that!" growled Padmos. "You sound like an imbecile. Is this how you want to die, mewling like a baby?"

"Waaaaahhhhh!" cried Daman in response.

"Fool!" hissed Padmos.

Boric's hand went to the pommel of his sword as he imagined smacking Padmos on the back of the head with the flat of his blade. But no sooner had he touched the pommel than he jerked his hand away as if he'd been stung. "What in the…" he mouthed to himself. Brakslaagt seemed to be vibrating in its scabbard, as if it had been struck by a hammer. He peered at the pommel in the dim light, but his breath caught in his throat as his attention was seized by something moving underneath him. A hulking figure lurked directly underneath the bough on which Boric perched, barely visible in the moonlight. The ogre!

Even bent over, with its massive hands nearly dragging on the ground, the creature had to be a good nine feet tall. Forget about climbing trees; the ogre could easily reach up and grab Boric by the ankle without even straightening its torso. Idiot! thought Boric. I'm a sitting duck. It was only dumb luck that the ogre hadn't yet spotted him. A slight shift in the gentle night breeze, or a quick glance upward, and the ogre would have him. Boric didn't have a chance.

The giant beast reached its leathery hand out to the trunk of the tree, seeming to be taking stock of its situation. Its head craned back, cavernous nostrils sniffing the night air. Boric thought he saw the creature's brow furl in perplexity. It smells me, he thought. It just can't pinpoint my location. Boric considered drawing his sword, but he didn't dare move. The smallest sound would be like a claxon to the ogre.

"Boric!" called Padmos again. The ogre's head crooked to hear the sound.

"Waaaaahhhhh!" cried Daman. The ogre's limbs twitched with excitement at the wail. It seemed to instantly forget about Boric and lumbered toward the open window. For a moment, Boric lost sight of the creature in the shadows. There was a terrified screech followed by a bellowing roar. The bait had worked.

Boric swung down from the bough, landing in a crouch at the foot of the oak tree, and then sprinted toward the house. His hand brushed the pommel of Brakslaagt again, and he noted that it was still vibrating, but less intensely. Had it been reacting to the danger posed by the ogre?

Padmos screamed again. Ahead of Boric, the hulking figure of the ogre bent over next to the window, fishing around inside the house with its right arm.

"Pull the rope!" cried Boric. The ogre turned its massive head to face Boric, its arm still nearly shoulder-deep in the house. Boric heard muffled shouts from inside the house.

"Pull it!" cried Boric again. The ogre's face contorted in anger at Boric. Still fixated on the "baby" in the house, it clearly resented this intrusion. It bared a mouthful of crooked yellow teeth and pulled its arm from the house. It advanced toward Boric, but suddenly stopped short as its right arm jerked to a halt behind it: a loop of thick rope was wrapped around its wrist. The other end of the rope disappeared inside the house.

"We got him!" hollered Daman from inside the house. "We did it!"

Boric swallowed hard. He wanted to believe that it really was that easy, but he knew that he had underestimated the size of the ogre. What if...?

As if in response to his half-formed question, the ogre planted its feet wide on the ground, leaning away from the house, and then thrust its arm forward. Miraculously, the rope didn't break, but what did happen was arguably worse. Boric had secured the other end of the rope to what remained of the stone chimney that ran down the center of the house, and as Boric stared in awe, a sizeable chunk of the chimney exploded from the house as if the wall was made of paper, revealing two terrified men cowering inside. The fragment of stone and masonry sailed over the ogre's right shoulder toward Boric, who barely managed to dive out of the way. The chimney struck a sapling behind Boric, reducing it to splinters. Boric had to admit that as much as he disliked the elves, they made some damn strong rope. The cord was barely half an inch thick, but it was stronger than steel.

The ogre grinned at Boric. Boric smiled weakly back at the ogre.

Ogres are stupid, thought Boric. I can outsmart him. But another part of his brain retorted, Of course you can. Why, look how well you're doing so far!

The fact was, Boric knew, ogres *were* stupid, at least in most capacities. You wouldn't want to rely on an ogre to recount the Seven Ages of the Old Realm or remind you which of the wines of Swarnholme went best with lobster. But there was one thing that ogres were very smart about, and that was smashing things. For all their other intellectual failings, ogres were precocious smashers.

An ogre might never have figured out how to create an incredibly effective weapon by securing a rope to a five-hundred-pound chunk of stone, but by Grovlik, an ogre knew what to do with such a thing when it was presented to him.

And that's why the ogre smiled.

Boric got to his feet and brushed the dust off his tunic, glaring defiantly at the ogre. If he was going to die, he was going to die like a man.

The ogre wrapped the silvery elven cord around his wrist several times and pulled. The chimney lifted off the ground and soared into the air, whirling in a great arc over the creature's head. Boric gulped. As big as the ogre was, it was even stronger than its size indicated. It whirled the chimney faster and faster, seeming to relish its power over Boric. It had already demolished the only tree nearby; there was no cover within reach. Boric stood on the balls of his feet with his sword drawn, shifting his weight back and forth as he waited for the ogre to release the chimney.

The ogre brought the chimney around one last time and then stepped forward to send the massive chunk of stone hurtling toward Boric. Boric dove under the projectile, sliding face forward on the dirt toward the ogre. The chimney missed him by inches, thudding to the ground where he had been standing less than a second before. Boric sprang to his feet and stabbed at the ogre's groin, but the ogre took a step back and swatted at Boric's head with its left hand. Even this absentminded blow was enough to knock Boric off his feet. His shoulder slammed into the ground and he rolled into a defensive crouch, raising his Brakslaagt before him.

"Shit," muttered Boric, wiping blood from his chin. The ogre's arms were too damn long. There was no way to get past those oak-tree limbs to strike anything vital. He was going to have to do this the hard way. The ogre took a step toward him. Boric turned and ran.

Behind him, he heard the ogre laughing its horrible, shrieking ogre-laugh, like a pack of wolves in a hailstorm. Fine, thought Boric, as he put distance between him and the ogre. Have your laugh. We'll see who's laughing when—

He was distracted by a jolt running up his arm as Brakslaagt nearly vibrated out of his hand, and he lost his footing on the uneven ground. As he fell, gravel pelted his neck, and he felt a rushing of air. A shadow passed over him. Lying prone on the ground, he craned his neck to see the ogre's improvised flail retreating into the sky. The massive hunk of stone had missed him by an inch, at most. By Greymaul's mace, the ogre was fast. If it weren't for Brakslaagt's warning…

Boric got to his feet and continued running. In a few seconds, he reached the tree where he had perched earlier. He slid Brakslaagt into its scabbard and leapt for a bough just over his head, hoisting himself onto it. Behind him, the ogre chortled with anticipation. Boric turned to see the chimney hurtling away from him. The ogre grinned, knowing that there was no escape for Boric. He swung the chimney around again and again, until it was just a blur in the night sky. But Boric wasn't watching the chimney. He was watching the ogre's feet for the telltale shift of weight that signaled…*there!*

Boric swung from the bough, landing just on the other side of the tree from the ogre. The ogre's tiny, smashing-optimized brain outdid itself in making a minute change in trajectory to adjust for his target's new location but failed to accurately assess the ramifications of another obstacle in its path. Boric flattened himself on the ground and the chimney sailed over his head, but rather than soaring back toward the ogre, it arced sharply around the tree, wrapping the rope tightly around the trunk. The ogre, furious with the tree for trying to steal his new toy, roared with anger and leaned backward, pulling with all his might against the tree's grip. As curious as he was to see which would give first—the tree, the ogre, or the elven rope—Boric didn't wait to find out. While the ogre was still gripped with arboreal fury, Boric sprang forward, lifted Brakslaagt over his head, and brought it down with both arms, slicing the ogre's hand clean off.

Its burden suddenly relieved, the ogre catapulted backward, tumbling crazily, massive limbs flailing, its right wrist spurting great fountains of greenish-yellow ogre blood, finally coming to a stop as it crashed into the ruined house. What was left of the roof crashed down on top of it, and the ogre lay there for a moment, covered in plaster and burned lumber, its gigantic feet twitching spastically.

Boric didn't dare give the creature a second's respite. He ran toward it, but even as he did so, the monster sat up and began to crawl out of the rubble. It tried to reach out toward Boric with its missing hand, great sluices of ogre blood pumping forth from its wrist. Boric lost his footing in a pool of the slimy stuff, stumbling and sliding uncontrollably toward the monster, finally slamming awkwardly into the mass of tangled hair covering its groin. He nearly lost consciousness from the stench. It smelled like a sulfur mine filled with rotting fish.

Boric retained just enough presence of mind to be aware of the ogre's other hand moving toward his throat. Boric swung wildly with Brakslaagt, hoping to buy a moment to regain his footing. To his surprise, the blade sliced through the monster's wrist, severing its remaining hand. The ogre, apparently coming to grips with the fact that it had lost two important appendages, howled with rage and wrapped its handless arms around Boric's body in an attempt to crush him in a bear hug. Still off balance, Boric didn't have time to react except to suck in a great gulp of putrid air and tuck his arms into his sides. The ogre squeezed Boric tightly and Boric pushed back, trying to keep the creature from crushing his ribcage.

Hot ogre blood poured from the two stumps and over Boric's body, making him feel as if he were being encased in wax.

There was nothing to do now but wait and hope that the ogre passed out from blood loss before Boric died from asphyxiation. Boric had once held his breath for four minutes in the icy water of the River Ytrisk, having lost a bet between his two older brothers, but this was different: Boric was already out of breath from the melee, and the foul air burned his throat and lungs. He was on the verge of losing consciousness, and when he did, his muscles would slacken and the ogre would crush his ribs like twigs. He knew he couldn't last much longer, and the ogre, despite its copious blood loss, showed no sign of weakening. In the distance, just before his eyes closed, Boric thought he saw the silvery silhouette of a wyndbahr approaching, its massive wings fluttering in the moonlight.

Then suddenly the monster's grip slackened. Boric filled his lungs with air and pushed the ogre's arms away. He tumbled to the ground and skittered away from the unconscious creature. Brakslaagt, still clutched in his right hand, was at rest: the danger had passed. The Ogre of Chathain was dead.

Getting shakily to his feet, covered with slimy, smelly ogre blood, Boric saw a blade protruding from the monster's chest. Behind the prone creature stood Daman the blacksmith. He had skewered the ogre with Boric's sword. Padmos stood next to him, smiling grimly.

"Thanks," said Boric.

"Don't mention it," said the blacksmith. "Now, about the three gold coins you owe each of us…"

"One gold," said Boric.

"Fairly certain it was three," said Daman.

"Two," offered Boric.

"Deal," said the blacksmith.

Exhausted, the three men made their way back to town.

# Nine

It was a sign of how disconcerting his whole predicament was that it wasn't until the dim gray light of predawn began to gather over the Kalvan Mountains that it occurred to Boric he had no idea who was now King of Ytrisk.

Boric had no sons, and in any case his father had established that it was the king's prerogative to select his own successor. Understandably paranoid, Boric had developed a habit of altering his selection every few weeks, entrusting various advisors with different versions of his last will and testament, each supplanting the previous version. This made it virtually impossible for anyone to guess who the rightful successor was and correspondingly reduced the incentive for anyone to assassinate Boric. The plan had been so successful—right up to his actual assassination—that Boric himself could not say with any certainty who he had picked to be his heir. One of his nephews, he thought. Or maybe that cousin with the clubfoot. He wracked his brain, but couldn't remember whom he had settled on most recently.

Had whoever it was somehow figured out that he was the heir and plotted to have Boric killed? (For there could hardly be any doubt that someone had bribed Captain Randor to stab him; the gold coins in his purse could only have come from someone who had wanted Boric dead.) It seemed unlikely that the heir could have found out about his selection, and even if he had, how could he be certain that Boric's choice wouldn't change between the hatching of the plot and its execution? No, whoever had bribed Randor had been waiting for that opportunity for some time. But who would want Boric dead regardless of his successor?

Brand. Of course. Brand had given him the sword, knowing that Boric would become his slave upon death. Monarchs of the Six Kingdoms didn't have much of a life expectancy; Brand probably never figured Boric would live another twenty years. He had grown impatient and had Boric killed. Boric swore once again to have his vengeance on Brand, whatever that required him to do.

But that left the question: who reigned in Brobdingdon? There was no way of knowing for sure without returning to Ytrisk, a course of action that was out of the question. Dead kings were honored in the Six Kingdoms only insofar as they had the good sense to stop walking around above ground. By the same token, Boric realized, he should be beyond concerns about political intrigues. What was it to him who the new King of Ytrisk was? No matter who it was, he would be no ally of Boric's at this point. All of the living were his enemies; his only allies were the dead. Perhaps he should have gone with the other wraiths when they had come for him at the witch's house. What was he trying to accomplish by wandering through the hinterlands alone, a dead man disowning his own?

Peering into the distance, Boric saw what looked like a small grove of trees. Shelter. And he might just be able to make it there before dawn.

"Who are you?" asked a small voice, startling Boric. He looked around, but couldn't find the source of it. Drawing his sword, he demanded, "Who speaks? Show yourself!"

But there was no one to be seen. Boric peered into the gloom, his uncanny vision revealing a stark gray landscape of grasses and shrubs.

"Where are you going?" asked the voice again, now behind him.

Boric whirled to face the intruder, but still there was no one to be found. "I command you to show yourself!" Boric growled. "I am Boric, King—" He broke off, remembering that he was no longer king of anything, and that it probably would not be in his interests to reveal that he once had been.

"Where are you going, Boricking?" asked the voice, now on his left. Boric turned and charged, thrusting with Brakslaagt. But his sword pierced only air, and his right foot struck something, sending him sprawling into the shrubbery. He scrambled to his feet, taking a defensive crouch—not that it would help against an enemy who was apparently invisible and could move like lightning and in complete silence. He spun wildly in a vain hope to catch the interloper darting from one bush to another, but still he saw nothing. To his left, the streaks of pink began to dart across the horizon. The only visible shelter from the sun was the small grove of trees a few hundred yards down the path. Already the light was piercing Boric's skull. As much as he hated running from a fight, he didn't dare remain in the open any longer. He sheathed his sword and ran, reaching the grove just as the sun broke the horizon. Boric sat down with his back against the trunk of the tree, wrapping his cape around him to ward off the light filtering through the thick canopy of leaves.

Boric found himself again wishing he were capable of sleep, but the corollary of being immune to exhaustion was the inability to escape his condition in the blessed embrace of sleep. For Boric, there was no longer any day and night, just an endless waking nightmare punctuated with periods of intolerable, burning glare. So he sat and waited in the little grove for nightfall.

"What are you doing, Boricking?" asked the voice from behind him, causing Boric to quite literally jump nearly out of his skin.

Helpless to do much of anything besides cower in shadow, Boric found his anger turning to resigned desperation. "It's just Boric, not Boricking," he said. "Please, who are you?"

"Chad," said the voice.

Boric wasn't sure he had heard correctly. "Did you say Chad? What kind of name is Chad?"

"What kind of name is Boricking? What are you hiding from?"

"Boric," said Boric again. "I'm not hiding. I'm seeking shelter from the light. What are *you* hiding from?"

A small person stepped out from behind a bush to Boric's left. He wore brown trousers, a green cotton shirt, and a leather jerkin. His head and feet were bare. From his size, Boric would have thought him a child, but he had the face of a young adult and he was built like a middle-aged man. He stood roughly half the height of an average human male.

Boric was stunned. He had of course heard stories about the diminutive people who lived to the east of Skaal, but he had never believed them. "Why," he exclaimed, "you're a halfling!"

The little man snorted in disgust, standing as tall as he could. "I'm a threfeling!" he said.

"A threfeling?"

"Three-fifths the height of a man. Threfeling. Why are you afraid of the light?"

"I'm not afraid of it," said Boric. "I...have a condition."

"A condition?" asked Chad.

"I have..." Boric stopped to think. The most obvious explanation for his behavior and the bandages covering his body was some sort of skin disease, but lepers were about half a notch above wraiths on the social acceptability scale. He doubted threfelings tolerated lepers any better than humans did. "...burns," he said.

"All over your body?" asked Chad. "How'd you do that?"

"I, uh, fell," said Boric. "Into a volcano. It's complicated. How did you do that, moving without me seeing you?"

Chad shrugged. "Threfelings can ought to move much more quietly than you lumbering onetutherlings."

"One…?" started Boric.

"One and two-thirds the size of a threfeling. Onetutherling."

"That makes no sense," said Boric. "You can't give us a name using a measurement that's relative to your size, when we've already named you with a measurement relative to *our* size. One of us has to be the standard."

"Well, then," said Chad. "I can should nominate us. Henceforth and from now on, we will can be known as men, and you as onetutherlings. Unless you prefer 'stomplers,' 'loudlings,' or 'thudscufflers.'"

"Ha!" cried Boric. "You're hardly in a position to make such pronouncements. You're vastly outnumbered."

"Are we?" asked Chad. As he spoke, a score of small men stepped out from behind trees and bushes.

"Well," said Boric, peering through his fingers at the diminutive figures surrounding him, "I'll be a thudscuffler."

# Ten

The sun was just coming up when the three ogre-killers returned to town. The trio's tale was at first met with skepticism, but the skepticism diminished somewhat when Daman produced a pancake-sized ear from his satchel, and evaporated completely when an expedition returned from the miller's house confirming that it now contained a handless ogre corpse. News spread quickly throughout the town, and Boric was all but certain that news of the ogre's death would reach Brobdingdon before he did. He worried that his brothers would hear the news and conspire to disqualify him from the throne on a technicality, claiming that he hadn't been the one to deliver the fatal blow. If he could get back to Brobdingdon before the news reached them, he was confident he'd be able to prevail upon his father to make the just decision. Unfortunately he was in no shape to travel. Exhausted and covered in grime and crusty greenish-yellow ogre blood, he badly needed a bath and a good night's sleep. The bath he managed, but there would be no chance of sleep while the town was abuzz with the news of the ogre's death. Every resident of Plik seemed to be crammed into the Velvet Gosling, clamoring for details of the trio's adventure. Fortunately, Daman and Padmos were happy to take center stage while Boric sneaked off to a relatively quiet corner of the tavern to rest his eyes and lubricate his throat. He planned to weather the storm in the tavern and then spend the night in Plik, leaving early in the morning to return to Brobdingdon.

Boric had just nodded off in his chair when he realized someone was talking to him.

"...brains behind the operation?" the voice was saying. He opened his mouth to see a young man—just a boy, really—sitting across from him. The lad was slightly built, with soft, boyish features and neatly trimmed beard. He wore a dark green cloak with a bronze pin depicting a pigeon in flight—the uniform of the Peraltian Messenger Corps.

"I'm sorry?" asked Boric drowsily.

"The reason I ask is that it seems strange for a messenger to get involved in such an adventure. Makes me think you are more than you appear to be."

"Hmm," grunted Boric. He had sworn Padmos and Daman to secrecy; if one of them had spoken a word about who Boric really was, he'd take more than his gold back from them. But this visitor seemed to be doing no more than fishing for information. Sometimes messengers—whether of Ytriskian, Skaal, or some foreign stripe—sought out information that could be sold to kings or merchants, supplementing their meager crown wages. Each kingdom's messenger corps was the local remnant of the old Imperial Messenger Corps, and although the messengers liked to claim lineage from that ancient order, the truth was that these days messengers were often little more than transients, subsisting on borrowed goodwill and stray morsels of information.

"What can I do for you, brother?" asked Boric warily.

"I thought we could travel together for safety," said the boy. "My name is Milo, by the way. Which direction are you headed?"

"Derek," grunted Boric, giving the false name he had been traveling under. "Heading north. But I have no need for company."

"Companionship, then," said the boy. "The road can be lonely."

Boric raised his eyebrow at the boy, uncertain of what he was proposing. Milo was a good-looking and delicately built lad, and Boric wondered how he managed to travel through dangerous territories such as this without being attacked by bandits—or worse. Probably by making friends with other travelers, such as Boric. "I have no need for that either," said Boric.

Milo held up his hands. "Please, don't misunderstand me. I'm not suggesting anything untoward. Merely a traveling partnership on the way to Brobdingdon, assuming that's where you're headed."

Boric shrugged. "I can't prevent you from traveling to Brobdingdon," he said, "but offer no partnership."

"When do you leave for Brobdingdon?" asked Milo.

Boric said nothing.

"Perhaps you didn't hear me," Milo said, leaning over the table, allowing his cloak to fall open. "I said, 'when do you leave?'"

But Boric wasn't listening. He was transfixed by the sight before him: the tops of two perfect white orbs straining to escape from a tightly drawn bodice.

"You're not…" he started, forcing his eyes back to Milo's face. Now that he focused more intently, he could see that the border of Milo's beard was a little too neat, his skin too smooth, his eyes too much like two azure pools in whose waters Boric would gladly drown if only for a momentary touch of those—

"Boric!" barked the stranger, whom Boric was strongly beginning to expect was also traveling under an assumed name. She wrapped the cloak tightly about herself, breaking the spell.

"Sunrise," Boric managed to mumble.

The woman smiled behind the beard and stood up from the table. "Then I will see you at sunrise, Derek."

# Eleven

The most noteworthy thing about threfelings, other than the fact that they are indeed three-fifths the size of humans, is their utter lack of noteworthiness. This, along with their natural stealthy and secretive nature, explains how their existence has gone virtually unnoticed by the entire civilized world of Dis. Threfelings do not engage in wars or other noteworthy happenings. The most pivotal event in recorded threfeling history occurred some three hundred years before the fall of the Old Realm and is known as the Great Imposition. Legend has it that scouts of the Realm arrived one day in the center of the threfeling capital, Threfelton, and, not realizing the various mounds and burrows surrounding them represented the pinnacle of threfeling architecture, declared the area "Uninhabited and Suitable for Settlement." Upon the arrival of several hundred human settlers in the area, the threfelings picked up and moved nearly a hundred miles away, leaving nary a trace of their existence. Threfelings still remember the Great Imposition each year with a parade culminating in sack lunches and bouts of competitive grumbling.

Thus the arrival of Boric the Implacable in New Threfelton caused quite a stir. Who was this hulking onetutherling, stumbling into town draped with burlap sacks? (Boric had promised to go quietly if the threfelings would conceal him from the sun, and as Chad and his cohorts had been on their way to a mumbleberry patch, they had plenty of burlap sacks with them.)

"What have you done, Chad? Who is this?" Boric heard a voice demand.

"He's a onetutherling, Mister Mayor," said Chad, a note of pride in his voice. "We caught him skulking."[6]

"Skulking!" cried the mayor. "And covered with burlap sacks, too. That's *aggravated* skulking, if my memory of threfeling law serves me. Explain yourself, stranger."

"Sir, I didn't mean to skulk," said Boric. "I am only passing through on my way to—"

"Passing through!" exclaimed the mayor. "Impossible."

"Surely travelers pass through your fine country on occasion…"

There were doubtful murmurs. Apparently a crowd had gathered.

"No one *passes through* here," said the mayor. "We aren't on the way to anything. That's why we live here. Now, remove those sacks and let's have a look at you."

"No!" cried Boric, drawing back and clutching the fabric around him.

"He's afraid of sunlight," offered Chad.

"I'm *sensitive* to sunlight," said Boric. "I have a condition."

"The condition of being a dirty rotten skulker," muttered someone in the crowd.

"Enough of that!" snapped the mayor. "What's your name, stranger?"

"I am called Boric," said Boric. A pseudonym would have been safer, but he had already given his true name to Chad and

---

6  Skulking, it should be noted, is considered a very serious crime among threfelings, although it differs only slightly from acceptable pastimes such as lurking and sneaking.

changing it now would raise suspicion. In any case, the threfelings were so isolated from the Six Kingdoms that they had probably never heard of Boric the Implacable.

"All right, Boric," said the mayor. "Let's get you inside."

Boric was led into a nearby building, where he had to stoop almost to his knees to get inside. The burlap sacks were removed and a sudden glare blinded him. Making matters worse, his eyelids seemed to be stuck open. He held up his hands in an attempt to ward off the light. "Please, the windows!" he yelped.

The window shutters were closed and Boric sighed with relief. Boric found himself in a domed room that might have served as a pantry in Kra'al Brobdingdon, but appeared to be a sort of town hall. Small round windows, now shuttered, dotted the walls about halfway to the dome's apex, and several narrow tunnels ran out of the room, presumably leading to similar areas. Boric had the sense that threfeling architecture consisted mainly of digging out beneath hills and then shoring up the walls with twigs and stucco. Standing in the middle of the room, the ceiling was out of arm's reach. The mayor and several other New Threfelton functionaries were regarding him soberly.

"Now, if you would please hand your sword to the bailiff," said the mayor.

"Um," said Boric. "That's going to be a problem."

"Listen here, stranger!" snapped the mayor. "You are a guest in New Threfelton, and as such you are not permitted to carry a weapon. I don't know how they doing things in Stomplerville or wherever you're from, but…"

"You don't understand," protested Boric. "The sword is cursed. I can't let go of it."

"Cursed!" spat the mayor. "We'll see about that. Bailiff!"

The bailiff, a portly old threfeling wearing a sort of bronze cap, stepped forward and held out his hands to Boric, a look of grim determination on his face.

Boric sighed and unbuckled his belt, putting the scabbard in the little man's hands.

"There," said the mayor. "Was that so…"

But of course the bailiff was unable to take the scabbard from Boric. If he removed it from the left hand, the sword would stick to the right. If he pried it from the right hand, it would snap back to the left. After a minute or so of furious struggling, he somehow managed to get between Boric and the sword, but then found himself hopelessly adhered to Boric's left thigh. With the help of several of the other functionaries, the bailiff eventually managed to extricate himself, collapsing in a pile with the other threfelings. The sword dutifully clung to Boric's leg. Undeterred, the bailiff jumped to his feet and attempted to pull the sword from its scabbard—also to no avail. Even with the help of five other threfelings—three pulling the sword and three pulling the scabbard—the sword wouldn't budge.

Boric bore all this with stoic good humor, not feeling that he had much of a choice in the matter. He couldn't leave New Threfelton in the middle of the day, so he was bound to be the guest of the threfelings, at least for the next several hours. If he had to spend that time with threfelings crawling all over him to satisfy themselves that Brakslaagt really was cursed, then so be it. Fortunately, as stubborn as the little bastards were, they finally gave up after nearly a half hour of various creative exertions.

"All right," said the mayor, folding his arms across his chest. "I have decided to allow you to hold on to your sword."

Boric bowed slightly in a gesture of thanks. "I'll keep it in the scabbard," he said.

The mayor nodded. "Good, good. Now let's get those wrappings off you."

A collective groan went up from the assembled threfelings, who were mostly lying prone on the floor and wheezing in exhaustion.

"Also probably not a great idea," said Boric.

"Another curse?" asked the mayor.

"As I mentioned," replied Boric. "I have a condition. The wrappings help to control it. Don't worry, it's not contagious."

The mayor shrugged.[7] "You are a strange man, Boric, even by onetutherling standards. What brings you to these parts?"

Boric hesitated, considering how much he should tell the threfelings. "I am being pursued," he said. "By others like me, similarly cursed. They share my condition and are convinced that I belong among them. I disagree."

The mayor's brow furrowed. "So that's it? They want you to come and live among them? That doesn't sound so bad. Why wouldn't you want to be with your own kind?"

"They are...not good men," said Boric. "The pain of their disease makes them cruel and violent. I am trying to resist such tendencies, and being among them would not assist me in that endeavor. Sir, I didn't mean to trespass on your territory, and as soon as the sun sets I promise to be on my way."

"Hmm," replied the mayor. He turned to confer with the other functionaries, who had managed to pull themselves to their feet. After a moment, he turned back to Boric. "You are an officially

---

7 The fact that diseases could be passed from one person to another has been well known among the denizens of the Old Realm for centuries, but somehow never penetrated the collective consciousness of threfelings. The resulting lack of prophylactic precautions on the part of threfelings (and generally filthy nature of the threfeling lifestyle, living as they do in muddy warrens along with countless farm animals) caused them to be constantly bathed in a veritable sea of contagion, which strengthened their immune systems and made serious communicable diseases almost unheard of among their kind. It has been observed by more than one historian that the unlikely survival of threfeling society over the past thousand years or so was primarily a side effect of the profound and wide-spread ignorance characterizing its population.

recognized guest of New Threfelton, Boric. You may seek sanctuary here as long as you like, as long as you abide by our local rules and customs, and pitch in as needed."

"Oh," said Boric. "That's very kind of you, but really, I hadn't planned on staying very long. I need to keep moving."

"Where will you go?"

Boric said nothing. Where *would* he go? Thus far he had only thought to put as much ground between him and the other wraiths as possible. But eventually he would run out of ground. To the south and east lay the territory of the Lemani barbarian tribes, who would be even less welcoming of a wraith than the civilized kingdoms. To the west was the hostile Kingdom of Skaal, and to the east, beyond the Kalvan mountains, was the Kingdom of Blinsk. He would find no sanctuary in any of these places.

"Well, until you figure out where you are headed, you will stay here. It will do you some good to rest and get some food in your belly."

Boric grunted, fighting a wave of nausea at the thought of his exposure to rabbit stew.

"I have all the food I need," he said. "I would be much obliged if you could find me a dark, quiet place where I could rest, however."

The mayor instructed Chad to find such a place, and they settled on a dank, mostly empty cellar connected to the town hall. Chad begged him to consider a more comfortable room, but Boric insisted that the cellar was perfect. "But..." Chad protested. "It's like a tomb in here!"

Boric grunted and closed the door. He was alone in the darkness.

# Twelve

Boric regretted agreeing to travel with Milah—that was her name—almost immediately. She peppered him constantly with questions about the ogre, and about Brobdingdon, and about the Vorgal tribes to the north, and on and on. Her curiosity seemed to know no bounds. After several hours he realized that he still knew virtually nothing about Milah.

"Why were you traveling that way, disguised as a messenger?" he asked.

Milah smiled coyly. The road north of Plik was wide enough for two horses side by side, and she took advantage of this by riding along Boric's right side. She still wore the messenger's uniform but had removed the beard and wore her hair in braids. When they passed other travelers, she would pull her hood over her head and let Boric do the talking. She would have made a pleasant traveling companion if she had just shut up for five minutes. "I might ask you the same thing, Derek," she said.

"I assure you my beard is quite real," said Boric.

"But you're no more a messenger than I am."

"What makes you say that?"

"You talk like an aristocrat. You try not to, but you slip into it when you forget yourself." She contorted her face into a mockery of

Boric's stolid demeanor. "I assure you my beard is quite real," she growled, dropping her voice an octave.

Boric scowled.

"Cease your prattling, wench!" she went on.

Boric found himself smiling in spite of himself.

"I assure you that my sword is quite long!" she growled.

Boric broke into a laugh. "All right, enough," he said. "It's true, I'm not a messenger. I am the son of a nobleman from Brobdingdon. My father is quite wealthy, but as the third of three sons I don't stand to inherit much. The king offered a reward for killing the ogre, and I volunteered." This account was true, of course, although it left out some important details.

"I knew it!" said Milah.

"Your turn," said Boric. "Why are you traveling as a messenger?"

"Because I *am* a messenger. Check the official rolls. Milo of Skaal."

"You signed up for the Messenger Corps under an assumed name?"

"I had to. They don't accept girls."

"Because it isn't safe for a girl to travel alone."

"I've done all right," she said, patting the pommel of her sword. "Been on the road for over a year now."

"You've been lucky," said Boric.

"I've been careful," she replied. "In any case, I'm almost done."

"Done?"

"Brobdingdon is my last stop. I have one last message to deliver, to King Toric."

Boric's eyebrow raised at the mention of his father. He would have asked Milah who the message was from, but telling him would violate the messengers' code of conduct.

"You know the king?" she asked.

"I've met him," said Boric.

"I hear he is a wise man, but that his sons are cowards and fools. Is that true?"

"It's mostly true," Boric admitted.

"Does your father have any... influence with the king?"

"My father?"

"You said your father was a wealthy nobleman."

"Well, yes, I suppose the king has taken advice from my father from time to time."

Milah clenched her fists in the air. "Yes!" she exclaimed. "I knew it! This is the one! It's finally going to happen! Why didn't I go to Ytrisk first? People said that it was a backward province, that the king didn't have the money and wouldn't see the value, so I wasted a year traveling to the other five kingdoms. And it turns out I should have gone to Ytrisk first! But then I might not have met you, and obviously our meeting was meant to happen. So that you could take me to your father, and he could talk to the king!" She squealed with excitement.

Boric regarded her, puzzled.

"My message," she explained. "It's not really a message. I mean, it is. It's a message from me. About an opportunity. Something that could change the world. My father, you see, was one of the court alchemists in Avaress. He was killed in one of the barbarian invasions after the Fall, but his notes survived. My older brother inherited his laboratory, but he had no interest in alchemy. I've always been fascinated with it, though, ever since I was a kid. A few years ago I started reading my father's notes and I realized what he was trying to do and how close he was when he died. I convinced my brother to allow me to continue his work. The deal was that if I succeeded, he was going to go to the King of Avaress and try to get funding."

"Funding? What do you mean by funding?"

"Well, I could only create a single prototype, and it didn't work very well. The idea was to sell the king on the idea, and get him to build us a much bigger laboratory and supply us with the minerals that we needed—"

"Milah, slow down," said Boric. "A prototype of what?"

Excitement shone in Milah's eyes. "I'll show you." She halted her horse and dismounted, pulling the beast to the side of the road. Boric did the same. Reaching into her pack, she pulled out something, wrapped in cloth and string. She untied the string and unwrapped the cloth. Inside were two discs about the thickness of a coin and the width of Boric's palm. She handed one to Boric.

"What is it?" Boric asked.

"Look at it," said Milah.

Boric looked at the disc. One side was dull gray and the other was glossy silver, almost like a mirror, but the image it showed was dark and blurry. "A mirror?" asked Boric. "I can hardly see myself in it."

"It's not you," said Milah. "It's me." She was holding her own mirror in front of her face.

Boric squinted at the mirror. "If you say so. What's the point?"

"It's a two-way mirror!" Milah exclaimed excitedly. "I can see you and you can see me!"

"All I see is a blur," said Boric dubiously, cocking his head. "It looks a little like a monkey."

"Well, like I said, this is a prototype. The zelaznium isn't pure enough to get a good picture. I need a bigger lab and better equipment, and—"

"The what?"

"Oh, it's what the mirror is made of. A mineral called zelaznium. I named it after my father, Zelaznus. He's the one who discovered it. The final version will be bigger, of course, and much clearer. And it will have a significantly longer range. These only work over about twenty feet. But with better equipment and purer zelaznium, I could make a pair that can send images up to a hundred feet. Maybe more."

Boric frowned. "What's the point?"

"Communication over long distances!" Milah exclaimed.

"I can already communicate over a hundred feet," replied Boric. "It's called shouting. Anyway, I can't talk through the mirror, can I?"

"No, but you could use hand signals—"

"I can use hand signals without a mirror."

"Yes, but don't you see the potential? Maybe eventually we could string a series of mirrors together, or find some way of amplifying or focusing the transmission."

"Whatifying the what now?"

"Think of it this way: what would you do if you wanted to say something to someone on that ridge over there?"

"I'd yell."

"And if they didn't hear you?"

"Yell louder."

"And if they still didn't hear you?"

Boric thought. "Cup my hands around my mouth."

"Exactly! So I just need to find a way to make the mirror louder. And find a way to focus the transmission, the way you do when you cup your hands around your mouth. The principles are quite simple; I just need time and equipment and manpower."

"In other words, you need money."

"Yes."

"How much?"

Milah bit her lip. "A hundred thousand gold pieces would get me started, and say, another forty thousand a year for the next ten years or so. Plus a large supply of zelaznium, which would require—"

"*A hundred thousand gold pieces?*" Boric asked, amazed at Milah's presumption.

"Yes, well, now you understand why I've been going from kingdom to kingdom. Only the monarchs have that kind of money. First my brother went to King Rapelini of Avaress, but Rapelini is a paranoid miser. He turned down my brother's request but kept the prototypes he had been carrying so that he wouldn't be able to get funding from any of the other monarchs. My brother, who had no interest in the mirrors himself but knew they were my passion, demanded that King Rapelini return them. Rapelini refused. My brother made some foolish remarks about making another set of prototypes and aligning with another, more farsighted monarch and getting his vengeance on Rapelini. He was tried for treason and hanged."

"I'm sorry, Milah," said Boric.

"Me too," said Milah, shrugging. "That was three years ago. Fortunately, Rapelini assumed that my brother was the brains behind the mirrors, so he didn't bother going after me. I spent the next two years making another set of prototypes—the pair I am carrying—and then applied for a position as a Peraltian messenger under my brother's name, Milo. I had no money; everything I had was spent on making the prototypes. My only hope was to make enough money as a messenger to travel to the other capitals and convince one of the other five monarchs to fund my laboratory. I had naively thought that in general kings were wise, or at least more or less sensible, and that Rapelini had been an exception. What I found over the course of a year, traveling across much of Dis, is that Rapelini was an exception all right: he was the only one who saw any value in the mirrors at all. Not only did the other four kings refuse to fund my laboratory; they didn't even bother to try to steal the prototypes. King Skerritt of Blinsk called them 'worthless trinkets.' Of course, they knew me only as a poor messenger boy;

I can hardly blame them for not taking me seriously. But if we can go to your father and convince *him* of the value of the mirrors, and then *he* can talk to King Toric…"

"Hmm," replied Boric. "There are no guarantees, of course. I mean, it's true that my father and the king are close, but I'm sure the king has a lot on his mind these days, what with the threat from the Skaal—"

"I know, I know," said Milah. "But I have a good feeling about it. I just know that the king will see the value of the mirrors if only we can get your father to present the case to him. He would do that, wouldn't he?"

"Milah…" began Boric. This was getting out of hand. He had been convinced in a moment of weakness to let Milah accompany him on his return journey, but he had it in mind that they would part ways once they got to Brobdingdon. At some point he was going to have to tell her that his father was the king and that it was unreasonable to expect him to introduce her to him so that she could try to sell him on some crazy scheme to make magical mirrors. Boric was going to have his hands full with his scheming brothers when he got back; he couldn't be championing the futile causes of some woman he had just met.

"I know, one thing at a time," said Milah. "I'm just a naturally optimistic person. I've had to be, to survive the number of rejections I've received. I just can't believe that meeting you was an accident. There has to be a reason. Anyway, let's get going." She got back on her horse and Boric, not knowing what to say, mounted his.

They rode the next several miles in silence. Whenever Boric looked over at Milah, she was smiling. It made Boric want to smile too. The women he had met at Kra'al Brobdingdon—mostly the daughters of other Ytriskian noblemen—possessed the intellectual curiosity and verve that came from spending one's days being schooled in important matters like which fork to use for eating fish as well as the bland homeliness that came from generations of inbreeding. A general rule seemed to hold throughout the Six Kingdoms that the more notable one's family was, the more plain looking and dimwitted one was likely to be. This axiom was so reliable that no one was surprised when a local idiot who appeared at the gate of Kra'al Brobdingdon one day, wearing an ornate horse blanket that he had stolen and fashioned as a sort of toga, was admitted into the castle by the guards, who assumed that he was an important member of the royal family. Boric and his father, being both clever and handsome, were exceptions to this rule, but his brothers took after their mother Gulbayna, a dull-witted, barrel-shaped hag with hands like ham hocks and teeth like the moss-covered boulders strewn about the bed of the River Ytrisk. Toric had married her in an attempt to secure the support of the semicivilized barbarian tribe known as the Vorgals, the chief of which was Gulbayna's father. Whatever credit Toric deserved for introducing some fresh blood into the royal line by marrying a barbarian's daughter was more than blotted out by his choice of a wife who was the result of an even more unrelenting regime of inbreeding than his own. Among the Vorgals, chieftains were selected on the basis of the number of different ways a man could trace his lineage to Stengol the White, the semilegendary seven-fingered albino forefather of the tribe. Gulbayna's father could trace his bloodline to Stengol through no fewer than seventy-two paths, making him his own uncle, brother-in-law, and nephew. Gulbayna was the fruit of Stengol's marriage to his half-sister/cousin, and the entire tribe was relieved when Toric offered to take her off their hands. When Gulbayna's father died, the Vorgals enthusiastically endorsed Toric as their king, having realized that they had pushed their own system of selecting leaders about as far as it could go.

Boric eschewed the advances of the homely and simple-minded daughters of nobility, favoring the sturdy, supple, and quick-witted (if not exactly well-read) daughters of farmers and fishermen. There was no question of him marrying one of these girls, of course—if he was ever to amount to anything more than overseer of the pumice mines of Bjill he was going to have to marry a woman with at least some small claim to nobility. His brothers teased him that as the youngest prince of Ytrisk he would be forced to marry some toothless daughter of the chief of another barbarian tribe—or perhaps even Princess Urgulana of Peraltia, who was rumored to be seven feet tall and possessed of both the complexion and personality of a tree trunk. Boric shuddered at the thought. Yet another reason to make certain his father honored his pledge to make the son who killed the ogre his heir. As the future king, of course, Boric would face an even narrower pool of eligible candidates. He supposed he'd end up with Princess Jaleena of Avaress or Princess Schmuske of Blinsk. But that was all in the future. There was still time to play. Milah was as hale and pretty as any of the farmers' daughters he had met and precocious as well. Yes, she talked too much, but he could overlook that.

They arrived at the town of Tyvek, halfway between Plik and Brobdingdon, just before sundown. Milah had reapplied her beard and pulled her hood low to avoid awkward questions. Messengers often traveled in pairs for safety but they never traveled with female companions. The fact that Milah was herself wearing a messenger's uniform would only provoke more questions. Best to continue the ruse that she had started.

This decision prompted another awkward exchange, however. Messengers were notoriously thrifty; they rarely had two silver coins to rub together. Generally during a layover they slept in the common room of the local inn, although it wasn't unheard of for a messenger to pay for a private room. Boric wasn't about to spend the night in a crowded room packed with drunks and ruffians, and he could hardly expect Milah to. But two messengers traveling together and sleeping in separate rooms would definitely seem an anomaly. This close to the capital it wouldn't be inconceivable for someone to recognize Boric if he called attention to himself—and that would raise questions about his companion. All he needed was for his brothers to get hold of rumor of him fornicating with a commoner while on an important mission from the crown.[8] So in order to avoid drawing attention to himself, Boric paid for a single room, assuring Milah that he would sleep on the floor.

He needn't have bothered. He had barely closed the door when she had pushed him onto the bed, unstrapped his sword, and began pulling off his boots.

"Milah, wait," he protested. "I have something to tell you about my father…"

"I don't really want to hear about your father right now," said Milah, removing her cloak and shirt. Underneath was a laced bodice that seemed to be padded below her bosom, making her shape more mannish. She appeared significantly less mannish with each loosening of the laces.

"It's just, what I told you about my father…"

Milah paused on the verge of removing the bodice. "Did you lie to me?" she asked, with sudden sternness.

"No!" cried Boric. "But I didn't tell you everything."

"Oh," said Milah. "Well, there will be time for that." She pulled off the bodice and climbed on top of Boric.

"Okay," said Boric. "If you're sure you don't mind…"

"Shhh," said Milah. "You talk too much."

---

8  Boric was always very careful not to let his brothers find out about his dalliances in Brobdingdon, knowing that they would use any evidence of fornication against him. This was sheer hypocrisy, of course: his brothers, not possessing Boric's good looks or charm, were well known by the proprietors and staffs of all the local brothels.

# Thirteen

Solace eluded Boric even in the stillness of the grave-like cellar. Lacking breath and a heartbeat, he found it difficult to gauge the passage of time, and meaningful rest—to say nothing of actual sleep—was an impossibility. Boric did not tire and he did not recuperate. He simply *existed*, forever.

No, thought Boric. Not forever. There had to be a way to break the enchantment. He wracked his memory, trying to recall everything he knew or had heard about the seven Blades of Brakboorn. He had spent some time after returning to Kra'al Brobdingdon researching the swords, but much of what he had found was—it seemed at the time—superstitious nonsense. He wasn't interested in fairy tales about magic spells and curses; he wanted to know how the swords had been made. What strange alloy—lighter, stronger, and more resistant to corrosion than even the best steel made by the master swordmakers of the Old Realm—were these blades made of? Who had made them? How had they been forged? When had they been created and why? To most of these questions he had found no satisfactory answers. According to legend, the swords had been designed by the Elves of Quanfyrr and forged by the Dwarves of Brun, but no one knew why, when, or how. Boric had dropped the matter when concerns of state became more pressing, content with the knowledge that Brakslaagt was a damned good sword. He didn't even know how old the swords were, or whether Brand had commissioned their creation or had simply come into possession of them after they had been created.

He was still pondering how little he actually knew about the Blades of Brakboorn when there was a knock on the door. "Boric?" came a voice he recognized as Chad's. "It's dinnertime."

"Not hungry," replied Boric.

"Erm," said Chad. "It's just that, well, the mayor is throwing a dinner in your honor. You should probably ought to be there."

Boric cursed to himself. "Where is it?"

"In the town center."

"I can't…"

"The sun has just gone down."

"Oh." That meant he had been in the cellar for, what, ten hours? It could have been minutes or days for all he knew. "All right, I'll be out in a moment."

The town center was, in a sense, the inverse of the town hall: it was a large bowl-shaped impression in the ground ringed by several massive oak trees. The center of the bowl was roughly flat and covered with a littering of straw. A dozen or so tables and chairs had been set up in the flat area. One of the chairs, a rickety assemblage of twigs that seemed to have been thrown together in haste, was nearly twice the size of the rest. Next to the makeshift chair — presumably custom-built for Boric—sat the mayor, and the rest of the table was occupied by the other New Threfelton functionaries he had met.

Dinner was not completely intolerable. Boric didn't eat, of course, but the light was dim enough that he didn't have any trouble pretending to eat while tossing his food to the stray dogs— some of them as large as threfelings—that ran unchecked beneath and between the tables. The threfelings ate as ravenously as half-starved dogs themselves, and soon the meal was over. Boric was about to slink off to his cellar when the mayor clapped him on the shoulder. "Wait till you see the entertainment, Boric!"

Boric groaned and made to sit back down. Visions of threfeling dancing girls appeared in his mind.

"No, no," said Chad. "You should ought to get up. They're moving the tables."

Indeed, the tables and chairs were being carried away and the crowd was fanning out, the attendees sitting in a circle on the grass slope surrounding the flat area. Boric went with Chad to the top of the amphitheater so that he could sit without blocking the view of any of the other spectators. When the flat area was clear, a sort of mobile stage, maybe two feet high and thirty feet in diameter, was wheeled into the center. A curtain hanging from a wire frame concealed the platform. When the crowd had quieted down, the curtain fell, revealing a small figure dancing gaily about the stage. It was about half the size of a threfeling and wore brown trousers, a green cotton shirt, and a leather jerkin, and carried a wooden bucket. It pranced around a cluster of small bushes, pantomiming berry-picking.

"Say," cried Chad. "I think that's me!"

Boric saw that it was true. The puppet was a likeness of Chad, with exaggerated features to make him recognizable at a distance. At first he thought that the puppet was being operated from underneath, but realized that the way it danced it must be a marionette. And indeed, he could see now that the puppet was suspended by very fine wires. But how was that possible? There were no rafters above. Where were the puppeteers? Peering into the sky, he realized that they must be hidden amongst the branches of the trees overhanging the amphitheater.

A burst of laughter from the crowd caused him to refocus his attention on the stage: another character, nearly twice the height of the Chad puppet had arisen from beneath the stage. It wore gleaming metal armor and its face was covered with ragged bandages. It carried a silver sword and was doing a sort of dance as well, in time with Chad but on the opposite end of the stage. The two characters hadn't yet noticed each other.

"And that's you!" howled Chad, poking Boric in the ribs with his elbow.

Boric regarded his likeness humorlessly. What in Grovlik's name was it supposed to be doing? The puppet was jerking about the stage furiously, like someone possessed. The crowd laughed uproariously.

Finally it dawned on Boric what the puppet was doing: it was trying to rid itself of its sword. The puppet was flopping its arm around, trying to let go, but the sword was obviously attached to the puppet's hand. Boric found himself grinding his teeth and letting out a long hissing sound.

After a minute or so of the puppets dancing around the stage, oblivious to each other, they backed into each other and leapt in fright. The two puppets spun to face each other. The Boric puppet jabbed at the Chad puppet with its sword, but the Chad puppet hopped out of the way. The Boric puppet hacked and slashed at the Chad puppet, becoming increasing agitated in its movements, but the Chad puppet simply frolicked out of its way. The crowd was in hysterics. Chad was holding his sides, tears running down his cheeks. Boric's hiss turned into a rumbling growl.

Not fully aware of what he was doing, Boric got to his feet and strode down the slope, leaping several threfelings with each bound. He jumped onto the stage and dove at the Boric puppet, which dodged his advances. Boric landed on his face and the puppet crept closer, menacing Boric with its miniature sword. Boric's arm swept out as if to knock the puppet off its feet, but of course this was impossible. The crowd roared with laughter and Boric pulled himself to his feet. If he had been thinking clearly, Boric would have pulled his own sword and cut the puppet's wires, but he could think only of the humiliation this accursed thing was heaping on him. He intended to tear it to pieces with his bare hands. But first he had to catch it—and every moment the puppet eluded him forced him to further involve himself in this farce, increasing his humiliation.

As he pursued the Boric puppet around the stage, he became aware that laughter was erupting from the crowd seemingly at random. Boric paused, peering at the crowd, prompting a new round of gales. He turned to look behind him and saw the Chad puppet mimicking his stance. While he had been chasing the Boric puppet, the Chad puppet had been chasing him.

Boric let loose a howl of rage. "You dare to mock me, threfelings?" he roared at the crowd. "You who share your dinner with dogs? You who live in warrens of mud carved into the hills of a land left behind by civilization? You runt half-breeds born of hedgehogs and goblins? I'll cut out your stomachs and feed them to your dogs! I'll rip out your entrails and strew them across your pathetic hills! I'll..."

He would have gone on, but he could no longer be heard over the crowd's laughter. Evidently they had taken his insults and threats as part of the performance. As he trailed off, the audience broke into a standing ovation. Whistles and catcalls echoed through the amphitheater along with shouts of "Bravo!" and "More! Give us more!"

For a moment, Boric's bony hand hovered over the pommel of his sword. How many of the threfelings could he slaughter before he tired or they put a stop to it? *All of them*, he realized with sudden horror. He would never tire and they could never stop him. He would just kill, and kill, and kill...until every living threfeling had been exterminated.

Boric jumped off the stage and ran off into the night, the cheers of the threfeling crowd echoing after him. He was nearly a half-mile outside of New Threfelton before he could no longer hear the crowd.

"Boric!" called a voice behind him. Chad.

"Leave me alone!" cried Boric, who kept walking.

"Why are you leaving?" asked Chad, running to catch up.

"I don't belong here, amongst the living. I'm a monster."

"You don't seem like a monster."

Boric stopped and turned to face Chad. "Do you know what's under these bandages? Do you know what I am? I could have killed those people. All of them. That wasn't an act, Chad. I nearly did it."

"I don't can believe that," said Chad.

"Then you're a fool, Chad."

"I know you weren't acting," said Chad. "You were really mad, I could tell. But you wouldn't have hurt anybody."

Boric grunted.

"It was just a show," said Chad. "They were just poking a little fun at you. It's what threfelings do. We don't can take anything too seriously."

Boric said nothing.

"You can leave tomorrow if you want," offered Chad. "But not tonight. If you leave now, the townspeople will think they did something to offend you."

"They *did* do something to offend me."

"Not on purpose. My people pride themselves on their hospitality. Featuring you in the play was just their way of welcoming you."

"Some welcome."

Chad snorted. "Boy, you're really full of yourself, aren't you?"

Boric glared at Chad. "What's that supposed to mean?"

"Where did you live? I mean, before whatever happened to you happened."

"A city called Brobdingdon, in Ytrisk."

"Do you have ogres in Brobdingdon?"

"Of course not. Once there was an ogre menacing the southern part of the country, but I hunted him down and killed him."

"Of course you did," said Chad. "Just out of curiosity, though, what would happen if an ogre showed up just outside of Brobdingdon one day, baring its teeth and threatening to kill a local peasant who was out picking berries?"

"I know what you're getting at," said Boric, "but this is a completely different—"

"For that matter, what would happen if *you* showed up in Brobdingdon, looking like you do? With your face covered and waving that sword around? Do you suppose you'd be welcomed with open arms? Or do you think maybe your friends and family would do something worse to you than feature you in a puppet show?"

Boric hung his head. Chad was right. He had no right to expect any sort of hospitality from the threfelings. They probably made him a guest out of sheer terror. What else were they going to do? In his defense, though, it wasn't the mockery that bothered him. At least it wasn't *mainly* that. It was that he wasn't entirely sure he wasn't just a puppet himself. Had he been acting on his own volition for the past few days or was this all part of Brand's plan? And what did his resistance matter if his humanity was rotting away along with his flesh, dooming him to be a soulless servant to Brand? But he couldn't tell that to Chad, of course.

"All right," said Boric. "I will stay for tonight. But tomorrow I must leave."

That seemed to satisfy Chad. They returned to town and caught the rest of the puppet show, which consisted of more parodies of local residents, most of which were completely lost on Boric. Afterward, he retreated to a dark alley where he could watch the night sky. He found it comforting to be able to see the stars moving across the sky in their predetermined paths. It was good to know that the universe's rhythms continued even if his own heart refused to beat.

# Fourteen

Boric and Milah left Tyvek early the next morning. The road narrowed after Tyvek, so they rode single file and didn't speak much. Milah seemed to be growing nervous about her meeting with Boric's father, and Boric was cursing himself for not telling Milah the truth. The truth was that his father wasn't some noble with access to the king; he *was* the king. And he didn't become king by throwing a hundred thousand gold pieces at every alchemist's daughter who rode into town with a crazy idea. Maybe if Boric vouched for her he could get half that amount, and he could probably spare twenty thousand from his own coffers, and then, with some initial success they could attract some investment from other... No! What was he thinking? He couldn't afford to spend either his money or his goodwill with his father on this girl's schemes. Even if she was successful in creating a much improved version of the mirrors, it would take her years. And how would it benefit him? He could see some advantage to being able to instantly communicate orders to officers miles away, but the army already had an effective semaphore system using flags, and when the flags couldn't be used, a runner could carry a message ten miles in less than an hour. The mirrors would have to be vastly improved to be worth an initial expenditure of one hundred thousand gold pieces.

No, Boric admitted to himself, his desire to help Milah stemmed not from the value of the mirrors but rather from the fact that she was a smart, pretty redhead with perfectly formed alabaster breasts. The thought of her breasts, in fact, set him off on a renewed attempt to devise some way of making her scheme work—or at least letting her down easy. If he could find her a nice house in Brobdingdon and set her up with some honest, respectable work in the castle—maybe as a scullery maid or seamstress—she might forget about this whole business with the mirrors. A dusty old laboratory filled with bubbling potions and whatever else one found in a laboratory was no place for a beautiful young woman anyway. With time she'd come to realize that, and be grateful to Boric for rescuing her from a life of fruitless toil. He couldn't marry her, of course; that was out of the question. But perhaps he could, ahem, *visit* her occasionally.

At some point, she was going to figure out that his father was the king. If she was as smart as he suspected, that point would be about three seconds after some Brobdingdon peasant called out "Hail, Prince Boric!" at the sight of him. Okay, so he would have to tell her before they got to Brobdingdon. He would explain to her that he had many enemies and was therefore traveling under an assumed name—which was true—and apologize that he hadn't trusted her with his secret. She would understand that, right? Of course she would; she had pretended to be a man for a year. She knew the value of deception. Then he would explain that his father was temperamental and old-fashioned, and that they would need to find another alchemist—a man, of course—to be the figurehead of the operation. Boric would find someone he could trust, someone who would pretend to have meetings with the king and reassure Milah that he and Boric had *just about* convinced the king to provide the money. They would drag this out for months, and meanwhile Milah would settle into her new life, get comfortable, and start to wonder why she had ever wanted to putter around a laboratory making mirrors. When Boric finally broke the news to her, she would just shrug her shoulders and dismiss the whole thing as the unrealistic dream of a child.

About an hour out of Brobdingdon, the road widened again and Milah came up beside him. "Milah," Boric said. "I have to tell you something about my father. What I was trying to tell you last night. He's... not just some nobleman in Brobdingdon."

Mila stared at him in shock. "You lied to me? You're father's not a nobleman?"

"No, no," said Boric. "He is. He's the *king*."

Milah scowled. "Don't mock me, Derek. I'm not some foolish girl who will believe anything you tell me."

"I'm not mocking you," said Boric. "And my name isn't Derek. I'm Boric, Prince of Ytrisk, son of Toric. I'm third in line to the throne." And hopefully soon I'll be *first*, thought Boric, if I can get to my father before my brothers poison his mind against me.

Milah's eyes widened in awe as she realized Boric was telling her the truth. "That's...that's wonderful!" she squealed. "We can go directly to the king then! We'll make the case for funding my laboratory together! How can he say no to his own son?"

This wasn't going the way Boric planned. How had he given Milah the impression that he was on board with her crazy mirror scheme? At most he had led her to believe that he would mention it to his father, whom she believed to be just one of many noblemen who had some contact with King Toric. Her faith in the compelling nature of her idea was clouding her sense of reality.

Boric explained to her that even though he was a prince, they couldn't just barge in on the king and hit him up for a hundred thousand gold pieces. They would have to develop their case and wait for an opportune time to present it. He didn't have the heart to tell her that he would have to find a more respectable figure to act as the figurehead of their project and that she was unlikely ever to meet the king herself. He'd have to break that to her later. She accepted what he told her with aplomb, but Boric could see the disappointment on her face.

When they arrived at Brobdingdon, Boric arranged for Milah to stay with a widow whose husband had been a long-time servant and friend of the king. Milah would be comfortable there and would have no direct contact with the king. Boric promised her he would return in a few days with word on the king's willingness to fund her laboratory. She thanked him cordially, and he went on to Kra'al Brobdingdon without her in the hopes of securing his right to the crown. He needn't have worried on that score. The king welcomed him with open arms.

"Boric!" cried King Toric as Boric entered the king's reception room. "The news of your success reached me just after dawn. The ogre has been slain then? The children in the southern towns are safe?"

"Indeed," Boric replied, bowing as he approached his father. "The creature is dead."

Toric smiled, motioning for him to stand. "Then I suppose I shall need to update my will."

Boric couldn't help smiling as he got to his feet. "I must say, Father, that I half expected my brothers would have managed to convince you that the ogre was a great uncle of yours and that by slaying it I was doing you a grave personal insult."

Toric chortled. "Perhaps a cousin of your mother's," the king replied, winking at Boric. "Do you take me for a fool, Boric? Why do you think I sent you on this errand?"

"Sent me?" asked Boric. "Begging your pardon, father, I *volunteered*."

Toric laughed again. "What choice did you have? You weren't about to spend the rest of your short life on that miserable little island, overseeing the pumice mines. I'm not as dense as you think I am, Boric. Neither of your brothers is fit to rule Ytrisk when I'm gone, but I couldn't very well pass them over without a compelling reason. Slaying the ogre was a test, a way for you to prove you were more worthy than your brothers. You each had an equal chance, and they chose to let you take the risk, hoping you would fail."

Yoric did more than hope, thought Boric. He had sent a servant to lie in wait in the stables and stick Boric between the ribs while he was picking a horse for his journey. If the man hadn't been suffering from hay fever and sneezed at an inopportune time, Boric might be dead. He would have liked to see the man put on trial, but in his surprise Boric knocked the man to the floor of the stable, and he was trampled by a horse that had been spooked by the scuffle. Boric knew the servant was a tool of Yoric's, but technically he worked for the king and Boric had no proof of their conspiracy. Rather than reveal that he knew about Yoric's plot, Boric had left the dead man to be discovered by the stable hands and let Yoric ponder whether Boric had killed him. He wondered if his father had heard about the servant and whether he suspected anything. Boric thought it best not to bring it up; Toric was, generally speaking, a just and intelligent man, but he inexplicably loved each of his sons equally. Boric had found that it was better to let his father come to his own conclusions about Yoric and Goric, believing that he would make the right decisions eventually. That reasoning appeared to be borne out by his father's decision to honor his pledge to make the ogre-slayer his heir. What Boric didn't realize at this point was that there was more to the bargain.

"I'm glad you're back, Boric," said the king. "Now that you're my designated heir, I have some matters to discuss with you." He gestured for Boric to sit with him and ordered the servants to bring them some wine. When the servants left, Toric spoke in somber tones to his son.

"You're a very brave young man, Boric. Clever, too. However, you are also vain, prideful, and occasionally very foolish."

"I beg your pardon, father," Boric replied, stunned at this sharp turn in the conversation. "Have I done something to offend you?"

"I received two messages this morning," the king said. "The first was of your slaying of the ogre. The second was of your encounter with Prince Corbet of Skaal."

Blast! thought Boric. Daman or Padmos must have spilled his secret and Corbet had caught wind of it. He probably ran all the way home and blubbered to his father, King Celiac.

"That fool was going to get himself killed, along with two innocent villagers whom he planned to use as bait," Boric said.

"Are these the same two villagers who assisted you in killing the ogre?"

"They are."

"And how did you use them exactly?"

"Well, as bait. But the salient point is that they survived and were paid well for their efforts. Corbet would have gotten them both killed."

"So you humiliated him."

"I beat him in a fair fight."

"Did you?" asked Toric, his face turning red. "The fight isn't over, Boric. When you picked a fight with the Crown Prince of Skaal, you started a war between Ytrisk and Skaal. Celiac has been looking for an excuse to take back the southern provinces, and now he has one. He's already begun amassing troops at the border."

"Then I will lead an army against him!" Boric exclaimed. "I'll beat them back to the swamp from which they crawled!"

"You will do no such thing," growled Toric. "The northern provinces are on the verge of revolt. I've had to send every spare regiment up there to keep order. We're in no position to muster an army against Skaal. Tomorrow morning I'm sending Goric to Skaal to lobby King Celiac for peace."

"Goric?" asked Boric dubiously. "Please tell me our hopes for peace with Skaal are not riding on the diplomatic finesse of that surly dolt, Goric. Send me, father. I'll smooth things over with that pompous jackaninny Corbet and his hairy baboon of a father."

"I can see that your heart would be in it," replied his father coolly. "No, Boric, I need you here."

"Here? Why? What can I possibly do here?"

His father smiled. "You can marry Princess Urgulana of Peraltia."

# Fifteen

Just as the predawn gloom was gathering in the east, Boric heard voices coming from near the town center of New Threfelton. Something in the hushed urgency of the voices worried him. He crept up the alley until he could make out the words. It was as he feared: more strangers with covered faces and bearing swords had been spotted in another threfeling village some ten miles to the northwest. There had been three of them, skulking about the town and asking questions. Boric realized he knew about the other wraiths before he heard the words; he could sense them not far off, the way one could hear a fly buzzing around a house. He had no sense of which direction they lay, but he had no reason to doubt the account of the threfelings.

"They're looking for me," said Boric, stepping out of the alley and giving the group of threfelings a start. It was the mayor, Chad, and the bailiff who had strived so heroically to deprive Boric of his sword. "It's all right," Boric went on. "I'm leaving. I think they are drawn to the sword. They won't stick around long if I'm not here."

"But they will pursue you," said the mayor.

"Yes."

"These men, they are like you?" asked the mayor.

"They share my condition, yes," replied Boric.

"Then they won't come after you in the daytime," said the mayor. "The sun is almost up now."

The bailiff added, "As of an hour ago, they were still in Farthington. I took a shortcut that they wouldn't know about and wouldn't be able to take on horseback anyway. I don't think they will be here anytime soon."

"So there's no point in leaving now," said Chad. "You can't ought to travel in the daytime. If you sneak out just before dark, we can should stall them—"

"Stall them!" cried Boric. "You'll only stall them for as long as it takes for them to run you through with their swords."

"No," said the mayor. "Boric, you are our guest. We won't have you fleeing for your life. You sought sanctuary in our town, and it is our duty to protect you from these men."

"Mayor," said Boric patiently, eying the brightening glare in the east, "I greatly appreciate your hospitality and willingness to aid me in my plight, but you are pissing against the wind, if you'll pardon the expression. These men won't stop until I join them. They *can't* be stopped. Even if you had weapons, which you don't, there is nothing that—Gaaahhh!" The first rays of sunlight pierced Boric's eye sockets, bringing him to his knees.

"Get him to the cellar," said the mayor. "And call a meeting of the town watch. We've got some preparations to make for our visitors this evening." Someone found a tarp to throw over Boric's head, and he was ushered back to his cellar for the day.

Just after nightfall three horsemen dressed all in black came riding into New Threfelton, ducking as they passed under the New Threfelton Arch, on which was inscribed the New Threfelton motto, "We Don't Want Any Trouble." The town was dark and the streets were empty, but the hum of their swords told them their prey was somewhere close by. They followed the main thoroughfare to the town center, where they saw a tall figure standing alone at the bottom of a bowl-shaped impression in the ground. The men dismounted and approached the pit.

"Slaagtghast," called the one who had been Corbet. "Join us."

"No thanks," answered Boric. "I like it here. Nice people, the threfelings. I may take up pig farming. Or become a shepherd, maybe. I understand the sheep here hardly ever commit suicide."

"Don't be a fool, Slaagtghast. You are a wraith. You have no place among the living. Your destiny is to serve Brand."

"Make me," said Boric.

The three wraiths hissed as they made their way down the slope. When they had reached the bottom, they drew their swords and advanced on their prey. The lone figure retreated a few paces, but the three wraiths spread out to prevent his escape. They advanced closer, until they were within a sword's length.

"Don't make us destroy what's left of your body, Slaagtghast. Your spirit is coming with us either way."

"You're going to have to take me in pieces," said Boric. "As long as I can stand, I won't be coming with you."

"It makes no difference to us," hissed the wraith, raising its sword and bringing the blade down just at the shoulder joint of Boric's armor, lopping off the arm.

"Do you yield?" hissed the wraith.

"Yield? Why would I yield?" asked Boric.

"Your arm's off!" said the wraith.

"No it isn't," said Boric.

"Then what's that?" asked the wraith, indicating the arm lying in the straw.

"I've had worse," said Boric.

The wraith sliced off the other arm. "Cease this foolishness and come with us!"

"I'm still standing, aren't I?" taunted Boric.

The wraith howled with rage and sliced at the figure's legs. But before he could make contact, the figure suddenly leaped into the air, disappearing into the trees above. The wraiths stood, dumbfounded, staring up at the trees. By the time they realized they had walked into a trap, it was too late. Dozens of clay jars fell from the trees, breaking into pieces on the hard ground and drenching the straw with oil. A second later, a torch flared to life, spinning and sputtering as it fell to the ground smack in the middle of the three wraiths. Fire engulfed them as they ran screaming, waving their arms wildly, blinded by pain and rage. They fell to the grass, rolling and patting at their cloaks to put out the flames. Still smoldering, they scrambled up the slope and disappeared into the night.

The threfeling puppeteers let down a rope and climbed down from the tree. Several of them grabbed rakes and moved the burning straw away from the center of the amphitheater. Chad felt in the dirt for a handle, found it and pulled. A trap door opened and Boric climbed out.

"They're gone!" Chad exclaimed. "We did it!"

"For now," said Boric, shielding himself from the glare of the flames. "They will be back. I need to leave now, while they are still recovering."

"Where will you go?"

"Tell them I headed south," said Boric

"There's nothing to the south but rocks."

"They may believe that I only want to get as far from civilization as possible."

"But you're not really going south."

Boric shrugged. "Tell them I am headed south. Don't put up a fight. If you tell them what they want to know, they shouldn't give you any trouble. They won't waste time with you if it means losing me."

"What's going to happen to you, Boric? Will you be able to find a cure for your condition?"

Boric shook his head. "I wish I knew. Good-bye, Chad. Thank you all for your hospitality." He bowed in deference to the threfel-ings.

"Good-bye, Boric. Good luck."

Boric turned and disappeared into the darkness.

# Sixteen

The Kingdom of Peraltia, to the east of Ytrisk, is the least populous, least powerful, and overall the least interesting of the Six Kingdoms, being composed of the provinces that were not particularly coveted by Ytrisk, Skaal, or Avaress. Other than being the home of several hundred thousand relatively comfortable sheep, Peraltia is historically best known as a stabilizer in the relationship between Ytrisk and Skaal. Whenever either of the two kingdoms became powerful enough to start thinking about finally putting an end to the threat posed by its rival, Peraltia would shift its weight in favor of the weaker kingdom—generally in exchange for some additional trade concessions or, in some cases, an outright bribe. Peraltia's military was not particularly large or formidable, its claim to having never lost a battle being somewhat undermined by the fact that its military had never *been* in a battle. Still, the ten thousand men goose-stepping around the Peraltian capital in tin hats were an X factor that couldn't be ignored by either potential belligerent. No one with any tactical experience expected the Peraltians to be able to mount any sort of creditable offense, but morale among Peraltian foot soldiers was reported to be so high that there was genuine concern on both sides that the Peraltian army wouldn't have the common sense to rout even when facing the prospect of certain massacre, continuing to advance until every Peraltian had been killed. Such an advance would have the effect of tying up a sizeable defensive force for several hours, tilting the odds slightly in favor of Peraltia's chosen ally. Anyway, that was the theory that was floated by tacticians on both sides of the Ytrisk-Skaal border, and no king had yet been brave or foolhardy enough to test it. So ever since the fall of the Old Realm, an uneasy peace punctuated by occasional halfhearted wars reigned between the two rivals—and meanwhile Peraltia made up for what it lacked in resources by extorting money from both sides.

The price of Peraltia's loyalty at present was neither pumice nor gold, but rather the hand of Princess Urgulana, who was widely regarded as the most unattractive princess since records of such things started being kept. Even Princess Stugnafska of Avaress, whose bust had been mislabeled as "Gurthan the Goblin King" in the Royal Museum for three hundred years without anyone noticing, is thought to have been quite a looker compared to Urgulana. Up until recently, it had been widely assumed that Prince Corbet of Skaal would end up marrying Urgulana, but with the revolt in the north the balance of power had shifted toward Skaal, and Boric had pressed the issue by giving King Celiac pretense for a motive to attack. Boric spent the two days after his return to Brobdingdon poring over charts and reports from field commanders, looking for a way to repel a Skaal attack without losing the northern provinces, but he came up with nothing. The only way to even the odds was to secure a pledge of assistance from Peraltia—and the only way to do that was for the Crown Prince of Ytrisk to marry Urgulana.

Having despaired of finding a way out of this morass, Boric's thoughts now alternated on two different paths: on one hand he was reassessing just how badly he wanted to be King of Ytrisk. Was it worth it if it required being married to a woman who was evidently about as attractive as a goblin king? He had never expected to be able to marry for love—or even for *like*—and it was pretty well accepted practice for kings to have affairs as long as they weren't too obvious about it, but he still wasn't sure he was prepared to be married to a goblin king. And on the other hand, he reassured himself that she couldn't possibly be as ugly as she was made out to be. He had never laid eyes on her, of course; she was only thirteen years old and never accompanied her father, King Gavin, on any state expeditions. The official rationale for her rare public appearances was that she was "delicate." If she had some condition that made her susceptible to illness, that would explain why she was never seen, and a princess who was never seen would naturally become the subject of lots of mean-spirited rumors. She was probably a perfectly lovely girl who had been slandered by cynics.

Having convinced himself of this—or at least having failed to convince himself to cede the reins of power to his shiftless brother Yoric (who would have married a she-bear if it meant being King of Ytrisk), Boric agreed to marry Urgulana. Not an hour after he announced his decision to his father, he was informed that the princess had arrived at Kra'al Brobdingdon. Evidently she had been stashed somewhere nearby in hopes of receiving word of Boric's acceptance of the proposal. It occurred to him that the Peraltians were probably worried that he might change his mind if he were given too much time to think about it.

Boric met Urgulana for the first time in the main reception hall of Kra'al Brobdingdon. He stood at one end of the hall with his father, mother, and brother Yoric seated behind him. Urgulana was escorted by her own parents into the room, which was otherwise empty. When he saw her, Boric let out a gasp that turned into laughter. This seemed regrettably cruel in retrospect, but at the time he was absolutely certain that his family was playing a joke on him.

Urgulana was a man. At least, she gave every indication of being a man, other than the fact that she was wearing a salmon-colored gown festooned with daisies. Urgulana's shoulders were so broad that her parents had to drop behind her as she entered the room through the massive arched doorway, and at six and a half feet she towered over Boric, who was himself exceedingly tall by Ytriskian standards. She had no bosom to speak of; all of her girth appeared to be in her egg-shaped midsection and shoulders like cast iron cauldrons. Urgulana's hair, which Boric assumed to be a wig, was a glorious array of golden curls that added another six inches to her height, making her an even seven feet tall and only further accentuating the impression that she was a man in drag. Her long, oval-shaped face contained a pair of thin lips, two bulbous eyes, and a crooked, pimply nose, in no particular order. A layer of makeup that appeared to be about a good half-inch thick had been applied in an apparent attempt to blot out her face entirely, to little effect. Whoever had first thought to refer to Urgulana as "delicate" had a dark sense of humor indeed.

And so Boric laughed, because never in his wildest imaginings could he have conceived of a woman who looked like this. A split second after the guffaw left his lips, Boric realized two things. The first was that no one else was laughing. In fact, everyone else in the hall seemed to be making a heroic effort to be as somber as possible, which made his laughter seem all the louder. Even his brother Yoric was quiet, although he was half-hiding a smirk under his hand. The second thing he realized was that this was possibly the worst occasion for humor in the history of the Kingdom of Ytrisk and that, therefore, the odds were strongly against this being some sort of prank. Boric managed to force his laugh into a sort of hacking cough that probably didn't fool anyone but at least spared some small remnant of his dignity.

He straightened and regarded Urgulana anew. She scowled back at him, which incredibly had the effect of making her look even more goblinesque. Boric bit his lip hard to avoid bursting into laughter again and approached the gargantuan princess. "Urgulana, I presume," he said, inadvertently spitting blood all over the front of her dress. She scowled again and made a noise in her throat like a wounded bulldog. Boric winced and did his best to wipe off the blood with his handkerchief. He succeeded only in smearing the droplets thoroughly into the fabric and eventually gave up, turning the handkerchief over and tucking it into the front of Urgulana's dress. This covered the bloodstains as well as making Urgulana appear as if she were preparing for a hearty meal. She slapped his hand away with one of her leathery paws and held it out for him to kiss it, which he did, reluctantly. "Enchanted," she said in a thick, nasally voice that sounded like a billy goat with bronchitis. "Likewise," replied Boric. Urgulana's hand smelled like lavender and pork chops. He marveled again that this was actually a woman standing in front of him. No, not a woman: a little girl. Urgulana was just thirteen years old! How much bigger and manlier might she get? As it was, Boric was fairly certain she could crush him to death with her bare hands. He had slain one ogre only to come home to marry another!

But if this union would spare the lives of thousands in a needless conflict with the Skaal, then it was all worth it, he told himself without much enthusiasm. He had better luck convincing himself that it would be worth it when he was king and could order his two idiot brothers to oversee the pumice mines of Bjill. We'd see who was smirking then. He wondered how many years his father had left in him.

Fortunately their one brief, agonizing exchange was about it for the pleasantries. Boric and Urgulana each retreated to their respective corners while their mothers discussed the details of the ceremony. Urgulana's father reassured her that Boric hadn't been laughing at her, and Boric's brother reassured him that there was no reason to think that Urgulana was harboring any unpleasant surprises under her gown. Her giantism, he told Boric, was almost definitely not caused by her being a pair of twins—one male and one female—who had failed to separate completely in the womb. Boric punched Yoric in the mouth and he tackled Boric, sending him sprawling onto the carpet. Six yeomen had to be called to separate them. Urgulana was heartened somewhat when her father explained that the two brothers were fighting for her hand.

The ceremony was scheduled for the next day—both because of the urgent threat of a Skaal invasion and because of Peraltian worries that Boric would get cold feet. Boric found to his dismay that he was under constant watch. When he asked his father about the yeomen lurking about the castle wherever he went, the king apologized and explained that the Peraltian king had insisted: Boric was not to be given any chance to escape. This fact did not have the effect of reassuring Boric about the arrangement he was volunteering for. He was also anxious about Milah; he hadn't had a chance to check on her since he had arrived in Brobdingdon, and now he would have to wait until after he was married—which would make their eventual meeting that much more awkward. The sensible part of his brain told him to forget about Milah; after tomorrow he would be married, and in any case Milah was just a poor alchemist's daughter. There would be no place for her in his life at Kra'al Brobdingdon, and there would certainly be no place for her silly mirror-making schemes.

On the other hand, there was a limit to how sensible one could be expected to be. As the crown prince, he would be expected to spend his days officiating over pointless ceremonies and attending all sorts of dull meetings on trade and taxation, and his marriage would be a sham foisted on him by interkingdom politics. Surely he could be forgiven for an occasional dalliance with a commoner. And he could hardly imagine that Milah wouldn't be amenable to such a relationship—he just had to convince her to give up her foolish notions about those damn mirrors. On some level she had to know that no king was going to spend a hundred thousand gold pieces so that some common peasant girl could play at being an alchemist. She'd already been turned down by five other kings, for Grovlik's sake! Eventually she would come to terms with the truth and then she and Boric would...well, not live happily ever after, exactly, but they'd make the most of the situation.

What Boric had forgotten about entirely while weaving these scenarios in his mind was a wedding-day custom that was observed throughout most of the Six Kingdoms, having been inherited from the time when the kings were provincial governors appointed by the emperor at Avaressa. The tradition was to allow commoners to come before the ruler of the province on the wedding day of his son or daughter and make any request they wished.

In fact, Boric was so preoccupied with worries about the wedding and its aftermath that it didn't occur to him that Milah might make an appeal to his father until she was standing before him on the raised platform in front of the gates of Kra'al Brobdingdon. He didn't recognize her at first: she was wearing a dark green dress, elegant but simple—probably a gift from the widow. Her hair was braided and pulled over one shoulder. She looked radiant. And she was looking right at Boric.

Boric sat next to his father on the platform, as was the wedding-day custom. A line of several hundred people snaked down a wooden staircase and down the street, where it eventually merged with the rest of the crowd: thousands of people who had gathered in front of Kra'al Brobdingdon to witness the goings-on.

Milah was still standing there looking at him insistently, as if urging him to say something. But Boric didn't know what to say. How could he explain even knowing who this peasant was? He couldn't very well admit that he had met her on the road to Brobdingdon and shared a room in the local inn. Princes could be expected to sow their wild oats, of course, but it would be in extremely poor taste to stoke suspicion about such a recent liaison on Boric's wedding day. Not only that, but if he admitted to knowing her now, that would shut the door on any future liaisons. She would be forever known as "the crown prince's friend" and watched wherever she went. He'd never be able to be alone with her again. She had to know that, didn't she? She couldn't possibly be so naive as to think that he was going to vouch for her here in front of his father the king and thousands of his subjects?

Boric averted his eyes and the king, growing impatient, growled, "My dear, there are three hundred other good citizens behind you. Perhaps you could be so kind as to grace us with your request?"

"Oh," sputtered Milah, shifting her gaze uncertainly to the king. "Sorry, yes." She fumbled in a leather bag hanging from her shoulder. After a moment, she produced a small, silvery object.

"Knife!" cried one of the guards standing to the side of the platform, drawing his sword. On the other side of Milah, his counterpart did the same.

Boric leapt to his feet, drawing Brakslaagt. "Stop!" he ordered, but it was too late: the guard on Milah's left had already begun his swing. Boric stepped forward and thrust Brakslaagt into the path of the arc, simultaneously spinning and kicking backward with his left foot. The first guard's sword struck his with a loud clang just as the heel of his boot sunk into the other guard's gut, sending him tumbling backward, gasping for breath. "Fools!" Boric hissed. "They're only...Milah!"

He watched in horror as Milah, shaking with fear, dropped two mirrors. They struck the wooden platform and began to roll in two different directions—one toward King Toric and one toward the edge of the platform. "Catch it, you idiot!" Boric shouted to the guard who now had a boot imprint on his belly. But the guard was too dazed to do anything and the mirror rolled right between his legs and off the platform, falling eight feet to the cobblestone street, where it shattered into a thousand pieces. The other mirror rolled to Toric's boot and fell over onto its face. Milah dropped to her knees, her face ashen.

The king bent over and picked up the mirror, examining it. "A gift?" he asked, puzzled.

Milah's mouth was open and her bottom lip quivered, but she seemed unable to speak.

"I appreciate the sentiment," said the king, "but your craftsmanship is lacking. This one is cracked as well." He held up the mirror to show that a fine spider web of cracks covered the surface.

Boric helped Milah to her feet. "Bor...Boric?" asked Milah.

"You know this girl?" asked the king.

"What?" asked Boric. "No, of course I don't know her."

"You called her Milah."

"No, no," said Boric, irritably. "I said mirror. I was trying to tell these dimwitted guards of yours that she was carrying a mirror, not a knife."

"Please, Boric, tell him," pleaded Milah. "Tell him about the mirrors."

"I can't," Boric whispered. "Please, it would do no good. You must understand." He felt in his pocket and found three gold coins. He put them in Milah's hand. "Take it. It's all I have on me."

"What are you saying?" the king asked. "What are you talking about?"

"She's disturbed, father," Boric said. "Guards, escort this woman to the street." The guards took Milah by the arms and ushered her back down the steps past the waiting throng. Cries of "Boric, please!" could be heard as she was dragged away.

"Well, that was odd," noted King Toric. Boric slumped into his seat next to his father, nodding glumly. "Next!" hollered the king.

Boric couldn't have said with any degree of certainty what else happened that day. At some point, he was fairly certain, he became the husband of a goblin king, but that wasn't the experience that was going to haunt him for the next twenty years.

# Seventeen

Having realized just how little he knew about the Blades of Brakboorn, Boric decided that what he needed was more information. And if there was any place in Dis that contained a clue about his curse, it was the Library of Avaressa to the northeast. He would break into the library and find out whatever he could about Brand and the blades. But getting there without being intercepted by the wraiths was going to be tricky.

Rather than head back north and take the east-west road to Avaressa, he planned to go through the mountains into the Kingdom of Blinsk and then head north. Boric knew that there was a pass through the Kalvan Mountains to the southeast, but he couldn't say within twenty miles where it was. The threfelings might have known, but he hadn't dared to ask them for fear that if pressed they would reveal his route to the other wraiths. Even if the wraiths split up to cover more territory, they were unlikely to anticipate him taking the mountain pass. Now if he could only find it.

He walked east until the foothills became impassable mountains and then turned south, looking for a break in the peaks that might indicate a pass. He hadn't found it by sunrise and took refuge in a small cave for the day. At nightfall he continued to the south, but still found nothing looking like a pass. Some time after midnight he concluded that he must have missed the pass and did his best to retrace his steps. Unaccustomed to navigating by the stars, he lost his way and only by luck managed to find a cave just before dawn. As he settled into the cave, he noticed a chalk drawing on the cave wall. His initial excitement that this was perhaps a sign of some kind faded when he realized it was the drawing of his brother Yoric fornicating with a sheep that he had drawn a day earlier: he had been walking in circles. If he had been able, Boric would have burst into tears. Instead, he lay down on his back and determined never to get up again. He was, after all, a corpse, and it was about time that he started acting like it. How bad could eternity be anyway? At least he wouldn't have to sleep next to Urgulana anymore (they hadn't seen much of each other over the past few years but still usually slept in the same room to keep up appearances).

Boric had experienced only about six hours of eternity when he heard a sound he had heard only once before: a great, rhythmic throbbing, followed by a rush of wind through the cave. He leapt to his feet. The mighty wyndbahr had alighted at the mouth of the cave. On its back sat the beautiful blond Eytrith. She slid off the creature and strode toward Boric.

"Nice cave," she said. "Did you decorate it yourself?"

Boric moved in front of his drawing.

"Still holding onto that sword, eh?" she asked.

Boric made a noise halfway between a growl and a hiss.

The Eytrith folded her arms across her bosom. "Hey, don't blame me, pal," she said. "I'm not the one who traded his soul to become King of Ytrisk. I looked into you a little after our last meeting. Turns out you are seriously cursed."

"Yeah," said Boric. "I know."

"My name's Viriana, by the way," she said.

"Charmed," said Boric flatly. "So am I stuck here forever?"

"Beats me," said Viriana. "All I know is that I can't take you to Avandoor as long as you hold that sword."

"But is this my last chance?"

"Huh?"

"You said you were going to return in seven days. It's been seven days, right? I mean, the way you said it, it sounded like I was only going to get one more chance. So is this it? Is this my last chance to get to Avandoor?"

"Oh," said Viriana, absentmindedly stroking the wyndbahr's neck fur. "I can probably get you another week. Nobody's asked about you yet; you're not really that big of a deal."

"Not that big of a deal!" Boric exclaimed. "I slew the Ogre of Chathain! I minced the Trolls of Trynsvaan!"

Viriana snorted. "That thing with the ogre was an assist at best. And trolls? Really? Nobody hangs their reputation on troll-mincing anymore. I mean, don't get me wrong, you've got a decent ranking. Eighty-seventh overall, I think. But you're no Greymaul Wolfsbane." She snapped her fingers and her eyes went wide. "You know what you should do?" she said excitedly.

"What?" asked Boric.

"You should try to *break the curse*!"

Boric wondered what the penalty was for strangling an Eytrith. How much worse could they possibly make things for him?

"I've been *trying*," growled Boric. "It's not exactly easy, you know. First, I don't know *how* to break the curse. Even the Witch of Twyllic didn't know. And I've got these damned wraiths chasing me, and I can't be out in the daylight, and this bloody mountain pass is impossible to find…"

"Mountain pass?" asked the Eytrith. "Why are you trying to find a mountain pass?"

"I need to get to the Library of Avaressa to figure out how to break the curse, and I can't take the road, so I've got to go through the Kalvan Mountains and east into Blinsk. And then I have to go north through the Valmac Pass and into Avaressa. It's going to take me days. Maybe weeks. And that's *if* I can find the damned pass!"

"Wow," said Viriana, frowning. "That sounds *boring*."

"I know!" howled Boric. "I've been walking for *days*. I'm sick to death of it. Even if I find this pass, it's going to take me more days of walking to get to Avaress. Just hundreds of miles of pointless walking. I never would have guessed it, but I think that the worst part of this whole walking corpse deal may actually be the *walking* part."

"Well, all right then," said the Eytrith. "Hop on."

"Wait, what?"

"Get on the wyndbahr. I can get you to Avaressa in twenty minutes. I'm heading that direction anyway."

"Seriously? Can you do that?"

"Sure, why not? I mean, Eytriths aren't supposed to interfere with what's going on down here, but between you and me, we aren't supervised very closely."

"Okay, but I can't really leave the cave. The sunlight…"

"Oh, because you're a wraith, right. All right, well, let me go pick up this knucklehead who's about to get himself eaten by fire wolves in the Wastes of Preel. I'll be back at sundown." She climbed onto the wyndbahr, which launched itself into the air. Boric lay down on the cold stone floor for another eight hours.

At sundown, Viriana returned as promised. "Okay, hop on," she said. "I've got a stop to make on the way, but you should be in Avaressa within the hour." She climbed onto the back of the wyndbahr and helped Boric get behind her. The great winged beast leaped into the air, soaring above the Kalvan Mountains. Boric held tightly to Viriana's waist.

"Hey, look!" she shouted.

"What?"

"There's your pass! It was just on the other side of that hill. Wow, I can't believe you missed it. It's so obvious."

"From up *here*, yeah," growled Boric. "Try walking it sometime."

"No thanks," said Viriana.

They climbed higher, and Boric was suddenly blinded as the wyndbahr soared into the blanket of clouds resting atop the Kalvan Mountains. "Can you see?" he asked Viriana nervously.

"Not a thing," replied Viriana. "But then I have my eyes closed."

"Well, open them, for Grovlik's sake!"

"Why? We're in a cloud bank. Don't worry, Bubbles can see. He's never run me into a mountain before. Besides, you're already dead. You should lighten up."

She's right, thought Boric. I'm a dead man riding a winged bear named Bubbles. What could possibly go wrong?

But then they dived back down below the clouds. "Now what?" asked Boric.

"That stop I was telling you about. I need to pick up this other dead guy."

"What other dead guy?"

"Clovis the Dragon-Slayer. He's number twenty-seven. Be nice to him, and maybe he'll let you sit next to him in the Hall."

"Clovis the Dragon-Slayer? You mean Clovis, the Prince of Blinsk? The one with the eye patch? He's never slain a dragon!"

"Not yet, no," said Viriana. "But give him a few minutes." The wyndbahr was now plummeting toward a rocky ridge below. Boric became aware of a tiny figure moving along the ridge. Behind him was a cliff wall into that was carved the opening of a cavern. As Boric watched, a massive reddish-gold reptile emerged from the opening, spread two great, leathery, bat-like wings, and leapt into the air toward Bubbles and his riders.

"Move!" yelled Boric. "It's heading right for us!"

"Calm down," snapped Viriana. "We can't be seen by the living. That is, I can't, and Bubbles can't, and you can't as long as you're on his back. So just hold on and shut up."

Boric was immediately embarrassed by his panic—the dragon hadn't been aiming for them, it had only been getting some altitude to pursue the man running along the ridge. Bubbles soared some thirty feet over the man's head and Boric got a good look at him. He carried a sword and wore an eye patch: Clovis, Prince of Blinsk. Boric noted that Clovis carried a broadsword of a type that had recently become all the rage among the nobles in Ytrisk: it had a simple, even ugly design, but he had heard that noblemen paid handsomely for them because of their superior workmanship. Boric had tested one once but found it inferior to Brakslaagt. Of course, at that point he didn't know about Brakslaagt's considerable drawbacks.

Boric had never met Clovis but he had heard the stories. Clovis had slain ogres, trolls, and at least one giant. He had not, to Boric's knowledge, ever slain a dragon, however, and the way his situation was progressing he was not likely to in the near future. The presence of Viriana the Eytrith did not bode well for his prospects. Eytriths showed up only when someone was about to die.

The dragon bore down on Clovis, opening its giant maw to release a burst of flame. Clovis's cape caught fire and he unhooked the clasp, letting it fall; it twirled like a burning leaf into the chasm below. He was running as fast as he could across the rocky ridge, but there was no place for him to go, and the foul beast was gaining on him. The dragon's next blast would incinerate him.

"Come around!" Boric shouted. "We've got to help him!"

Viriana shook her head furiously. "Can't get involved," she said.

"*You* can't get involved. *I* can do whatever I want. I just need you to give me a ride."

Viriana thought for a moment and then shrugged, pulling hard on the wyndbahr's reins. Bubbles veered sharply to the left, nearly throwing Boric. They made an about-face and soon were headed straight for the dragon.

"Get me above it!" Boric cried.

Viriana pulled up on the reins and the wyndbahr soared upward, arcing over the dragon's head. Boric couldn't help but shudder as they passed over the dragon's snake-like, watermelon-sized eyes, but the creature gave no sign of having seen them. Once above the dragon's neck, Boric drew his sword and leapt from the wyndbahr's back.

Gripping Brakslaagt's hilt with both hands, he drove the point of the sword through the dragon's scaly armor as he landed. The dragon jerked and screeched, throwing Boric to the left and right, but he held tightly to the hilt of his sword, which was sunk halfway into the dragon. Unable to shake him, the dragon twisted its massive neck around to the right, regarding him with its giant, unblinking eye. There was no question that the creature saw him now. It opened its mouth and let loose a torrent of fire.

Boric threw himself over to the left side of the dragon's neck, holding onto Brakslaagt with only his right hand. A wave of searing heat washed over him, and he smelled burning leather and flesh. Something very close to pain shot through his arm. He didn't dare look at what was left of it, but it still held on. Fortunately the dragon didn't seem to be able to turn its head completely around, or he'd be a pile of charred bones.

The dragon, still soaring through the air above the ridge, had completely forgotten about Clovis and was now focused on dislodging Boric from its back. It turned its head around to the left and blasted him again. Boric threw himself to the right, flopping crazily against the creature's hide as he still held on with his right hand. This time he smelled less leather and more flesh. His arm probably looked like a sapling after a forest fire.

When he still held on, the dragon changed tacks, whirling upside down to make Boric fall off. But Boric held tight to Brakslaagt—or it held tight to him, and while the blade slipped a few inches, the dragon couldn't glide upside down for more than a few seconds. Still, it kept trying, veering back and forth between the peaks of the Kalvans and periodically flipping upside down. Each time, Boric's blade slipped another inch or two, and the dragon wouldn't stop jerking and wriggling long enough for him to get any leverage. Soon barely enough of Brakslaagt was embedded in the dragon to keep him from falling off. One more flip would do him in: he'd fall a thousand feet to the rocky ground below, smashing what was left of his body into pieces. And Clovis would be on his own.

Fortunately the dragon was so preoccupied with getting Boric off its back that it wasn't paying much attention to where it was going, and just as it began another flip it crashed head-on into the same cliff wall it had emerged from minutes earlier. Brakslaagt was finally wrenched free and the stunned dragon plummeted toward the ground with Boric following close after. As the creature twisted and writhed beneath him, Boric caught a glimpse of Clovis directly below them. He had evidently taken advantage of the dragon's distraction to creep back to the cave opening, probably to pilfer some of the dragon's treasure. As Boric and the dragon accelerated toward him, he stopped and looked up, his one good eye going wide with shock and fright. With no time to get out of the way, he drew his sword and held it, pointing straight up, above his head. The dragon fell on him with all its weight, crushing him. Boric landed on the dragon's back and bounced off, hitting the ground with a thud. The dragon struggled for a moment, gave a plaintive moan and a puff of smoke, and fell dead.

After a moment, an apparition of Clovis crawled out from under the dragon's carcass.

"Wow, thanks!" said Clovis. "I thought I was a goner. Holy shit, look at your arm!"

"You *are* a goner," said Boric, examining the smoking, charred mass of bone and gristle hanging from his right shoulder.

"Doesn't that hurt?" asked Clovis, amazed.

"Not really," said Boric, inspecting his blackened, bony hand. "I'm already dead, like you."

"I'm not dead," said Clovis.

"Really?" asked Boric. "Then whose feet are those?"

Clovis turned to see two black boots sticking out from under the dragon's carcass.

"Maybe...somebody else..." Clovis started uncertainly.

"And how do you explain *that*?" As he spoke, Bubbles the wyndbahr landed with a gust of wind next to them. Viriana slipped off his back. "Ready?" she asked.

Clovis looked to Boric and then Viriana and back again. Then he examined his ghostly hands. "So I'm really..."

"As a doornail," said Viriana. "The good news is, you're number twenty-seven. Congrats, Clovis the Dragon-Slayer. You could sit next to Hollick the Goblin-Slayer if you wanted to, although I don't recommend it if you ever want to get your hands on any mead."

"Whoa, how is he Clovis the *Dragon-Slayer*?" asked Boric. "The dragon *fell* on him."

"He killed it with his sword."

"Are you *kidding* me?" Boric exclaimed. "That was sheer luck!"

"I don't feel very lucky," said Clovis, regarding his ghostly form dismally.

"*I* killed the dragon," Boric insisted. "Did you see what I did? I jumped onto a dragon's back and rode it all over the canyon. That has to be in the top five bravest things anyone has ever done!"

Viriana shook her head. "First of all, that wouldn't even make it in the top fifty. Second, that's technically an assist, not a slaying. Third…"

"An *assist*! You're going to pull that again? First with the Ogre of Chathain and now the Dragon of Kalvan? What do I have to do to get credit for killing something?"

"Actually killing it would be a good start," sniffed Viriana, patting Bubbles on his head.

"I don't mean to interrupt," said Clovis, "but what do I…"

"These rules are ridiculous," growled Boric. "I'm getting shafted out of two legitimate monster kills on a stupid technicality. An assist, my ass."

Viriana shrugged. "I don't make the rules. And by the way, calling it the Ogre of Chathain isn't helping your case any. It just sounds pretentious."

Clovis was looking around uncertainly. "Seriously, guys, do I just get on the…"

"*Pretentious?*" Boric growled. "You know what's pretentious? Calling someone a Dragon-Slayer when the dragon *fell* on him."

"Oh, and third," said Viriana, "you don't get credit for the assist because you're already dead."

"What? I risked my life to—"

"You didn't risk anything, you big whiner. You're already dead. Get that through your maggot-infested skull, Boric. You're dead. Dead, dead, dead."

Clovis shuffled toward Bubbles. "I'm going to just climb on up the, uh, bear-thing…"

"And how is it, while we're on the subject," Boric continued, "that Hollick the Goblin-Slayer gets such high acclaim? They're *goblins*, for Grovlik's sake."

"He single-handedly killed every goblin in Avaress," said Viriana.

"There aren't any goblins in Avaress!"

"Exactly. What in Varnoth's name do you think you're doing?" This last was directed at Clovis, who was awkwardly trying to climb onto the wyndbahr's back. Bubbles seemed to think he was playing and began to nuzzle the Clovis apparition affectionately. "Back, fell beast!" cried Clovis, falling to the ground and raising his hands in fear.

"Take it easy, Dragon-Slayer," Boric said dryly. He glared at Viriana, who stuck out her tongue at him. She hopped onto Bubbles's back. "Crouch, boy," she said, and Bubbles flattened himself against the ground. Boric climbed onto his back and Clovis followed. "Up!" cried Viriana, and Bubbles launched himself into the sky.

Less than twenty minutes later, Bubbles the wyndbahr landed on the roof of the Library of Avaress. Boric climbed down and waved good-bye to Viriana and Clovis the Dragon-Slayer.

"Good-bye, Boric of Ytrisk!" said Viriana. "I shall return in one week! Pray that you have broken the curse by then!"

"Yeah, yeah," said Boric. "Enough with the theatrics."

"Good-bye, Boric!" called Clovis as the wyndbahr took off. "Thanks for the assist!"

"Poser," muttered Boric, waving absently at Clovis.

# Eighteen

Boric did everything he could to locate Milah after the wedding, but she had disappeared without a trace. The widow hadn't seen her since the morning of the wedding, and Milo the messenger hadn't checked in at any of the Messenger Corps outposts within two hundred miles. The servants Boric had sent into the local taverns and brothels turned up many a pretty young redhead, but none of them were Milah. He issued standing orders to notify him if Milo checked in at any messenger haunts or if anyone caught wind of someone peddling magic mirrors in Ytrisk, but these orders resulted in not a single lead. She was simply gone.

Boric eventually settled into married life at Brobdingdon. He was relieved to find that Urgulana had as much interest in him as he had in her. Initially this was a bit of a blow to his ego; he had expected to have to continually rebuff her advances and explain to her that he had no intention of consummating their sham union. But it didn't take him long to realize that he fell well outside of Urgulana's preferences through no fault of his own. Urgulana's orientation was as definite as her appearance was ambiguous.

Somewhat unexpectedly, though, this fact gave rise to a wholly different sort of tension in the castle. His servants continued to turn up remarkable specimens of femininity whose tresses ranged from auburn to near-crimson, and Boric couldn't bear to let some of them go back to the inns and houses of ill repute in which they had been found. Being the crown prince, he had a fair amount of control over the hiring and firing of servants, and after several months the staff of Kra'al Brobdingdon began to take on a decidedly ginger hue.

The quality and coloration of the female servants at the castle was fodder for speculation and rumors but the only person who really seemed to mind was Urgulana. Her own tastes, it seemed, ran toward petite blonds with lean, almost boyish figures. Once Boric figured this out, he was able to negotiate a compromise with Urgulana that dictated that she was to have final say over the hiring of seamstresses and kitchen staff. It wasn't long before one could ascertain someone's function within the castle solely from a one's hair color, and it was not uncommon to hear within the walls of Kra'al Brobdingdon such odd utterances as "The new gingers are hopeless with cobwebs" or "My soup is cold; fetch me a blond."

Boric kept very busy over the next several years. When he wasn't evaluating the staff or officiating over some ceremony or meeting, he was mincing trolls or dodging assassination attempts by his brothers. His brothers' preferred method was poison; Boric's food-tasters had such a short life expectancy that they had to be hired from consecutively more distant lands where they were unfamiliar with the notorious nature of the position. Sometimes, however, one or both of his brothers would fall on him in some dark corner of the castle, attempting to cut his throat. Having grown up with the two murderous scoundrels, Boric managed to stay one step ahead of them, but after having lost count of the number of attempts they had made on his life, he finally went to his father to complain. King Toric, unfortunately, seemed to view assassination attempts as a rite of passage for future kings. "Why, one time my brothers locked me in a beet cellar for a fortnight," he exclaimed.

"I survived on nothing but beets and my own urine. I was orange for three weeks."

King Toric died of a heart attack on Boric's seventh wedding anniversary. The next day, Boric ascended to the throne and assigned both of his brothers to oversee the pumice mines of Bjill. This engendered a fair amount of goodwill among his subjects, who for the most part considered Yoric and Goric to be haughty, capricious, cowardly, and cruel. Their exile was also welcomed by the rulers of the other Six Kingdoms, who found dealing with the two brothers exasperating. During trade negotiations the brothers would often make ridiculous demands to amuse themselves, such as the time they demanded ten tons of cat hair in exchange for an equivalent weight of pumice. Bjill being the only source of high-quality pumice in Dis, the other kings found themselves in a bidding war, each endeavoring to determine how many tons of cat hair he could come up with on short notice, as well as trying desperately to find a secondary buyer for several million shorn cats. When not one of them could promise more than a few hundred pounds of cat hair, Yoric and Goric stormed out of the negotiations in mock disgust and spent the rest of the night getting drunk and laughing uproariously at their cleverness. In the meantime, thousands of Ytriskians went hungry for the lack of potatoes, which is what they had actually been sent to acquire.

So there was little grieving when Yoric and Goric were exiled to Bjill, and even less when it was reported three years later that Goric had been accidentally abraded to death in a pumice avalanche. To no one's delight, Yoric lasted much longer, succumbing to the Bjills only a few months before Boric himself died.

Boric spent thirteen years doing the mostly dull and thankless work of ruling Ytrisk. His days were occupied by boring, pointless ceremonies and even more boring and pointless meetings. The cachet of the king was such that people seemed to think progress was being made on whatever issue was bothering them if they could simply get Boric to hear their grievances even if there was absolutely nothing he could do about them. He met with the pumice miners about the horrendous conditions of the mines; he met with the bakers about the price of flour; he met with shepherds about the number of sheep that were falling into crevices (this was before the epidemic of suicide among Ytriskian sheep was widely known); he met with farmers about the lack of rain. The aggrieved contingent would go away feeling better that the matter was in good hands, slowly become more disgruntled over the next several months about the lack of progress being made, and eventually demand another meeting.

The only part of the job he enjoyed was declaring war on Skaal. He did it whenever he could. Sometimes the Skaal would antagonize him by raiding one of the border towns or confiscating a shipment of pumice traveling through their territory, but most of the time he was just bored. Declaring war on Skaal increased patriotism among the people, made them forget about all their other problems, killed off some of the excess population, often resulted in the acquisition of some valuable booty, and—most importantly—relieved Boric's crushing boredom. It was too bad about the killing, of course, but most of the peasants were probably going to die of plague or starvation anyway. There was a lot of that going around and not much Boric could do about it. And at least he had the balls to lead his troops into battle, not like some kings who kept on attending boring meetings throughout the course of a war.

Boric was popular among the other kings (except for King Corbet, who ascended to the Skaal throne shortly after Boric became King of Ytrisk). Part of this was goodwill engendered by Boric's father. Toric had been an honorable man and generally well liked, although his wife, Gulbayna, was considered uncouth and was nearly as difficult to look at as Boric's own wife, Urgulana. Fortunately, Boric seemed to take after his father both in looks and bearing. To Boric's dismay, though, his mother decided to take on the role of a sort of goodwill ambassador to the other kingdoms after his father's death; she did so much damage to Ytrisk's reputation abroad that Boric had to form a special diplomatic corps to follow behind her on her travels and apologize. Her death, five years after Toric's, created an international incident that nearly caused King Jeddac of Blinsk to break off all trade with Ytrisk: having gorged herself on the poisonous crayfish of Lake Blinsk, she fell into a well and rotted there for three days, sickening several hundred Blinskians. Only the finesse of Boric's diplomatic corps kept Jeddac from refusing to send any more salt or copper (the chief exports of Blinsk) to Ytrisk.

The resolution of the Gulbayna Incident—as it was called—was good news for Boric, because Ytrisk was still embroiled in an on-again, off-again war with Skaal and couldn't afford to deal with a trade war with Blinsk at the same time. Relations between Skaal and Ytrisk improved a bit after King Corbet died in one of the many Skaal invasions of the southern part of Ytrisk, about a year after the death of Boric's mother. Corbet had never completely gotten over his humiliation at the hand of Boric, and he always seemed to inject personal sentiment into the age-old conflict between the two countries. King Celiac and King Toric had always been at each other's throats too, but it was never personal. Declaring war on each other, burning each other's crops, and stealing each other's cattle was just what kings did. There was no call for bringing emotions into it the way Corbet did. It was unprofessional.

So it was a relief to Boric when Corbet was killed by a chance hit by an Ytriskian arrow in what was called by Ytriskian historians The Fourteenth Battle of Plik. The battle had no conclusive result (in keeping with the spirit of the thirteen previous battles of Plik), but the death of Prince Corbet at first threatened to escalate the hostilities between the two kingdoms even further: although Corbet had clearly been seen to fall from a parapet with an arrow lodged in his throat, his body was never found. The Skaal accused the Ytriskians of stealing the corpse, but the Ytriskians pointed out that this was obviously impossible: they'd have had to send men a hundred yards behind enemy lines and surreptitiously drag the corpse across an active battlefield. If they had men capable of such a feat, surely the Fourteenth Battle of Plik would have ended more decisively. The mystery of the missing corpse was never solved.

This was not the last strange occurrence revolving around the death of one of the kings of the Six Kingdoms. King Loren of Avaress, moments after being severely mauled by a wild boar in the southern reaches of the Thick Forest, got to his feet and staggered off into the woods, never to be seen again. Similar rumors surrounded the deaths of some of the other kings over the next several years. Boric dismissed it all as old wives' tales. He didn't know what had happened to Corbet's body, but then he didn't know where the sun went when it set over the Sea of Dis, what lay beyond the Wastes of Preel, or why potatoes were so damned expensive. It wasn't his job to figure everything out. It was hard enough just sitting through the meetings.

# Nineteen

Boric made his way to the edge of the roof and lowered himself through a window. The library occupied six large rooms in a temple-like building. Boric understood that it was essentially a diminutive replica of the original Library of Avaress, which had been burned during the riots after the Fall. The original library had been a vast structure with dozens of rooms, each containing thousands of volumes—most of which had been lost in the fire. Many of the books in the new library had singed covers, and one entire room was filled with fragments of books that still needed to be reassembled and bound. There were desks where scribes could work, filling in gaps of books from copies, many of which had been borrowed from the libraries of the other five kingdoms. Boric himself had recently given approval for a temporary trade of some fifty volumes from the Brobdingdon Library to Avaressa. The process of recovering knowledge that had been lost in the Fall was laborious and time consuming; it had been going on since the Rise of the Six Kingdoms and, given the paltry resources dedicated to it, would probably take another hundred years. Even then, it would be incomplete: there had been only one copy of many of the books that were destroyed.

Boric spent the rest of the night poring through ancient books, looking for information on the Seven Blades of Brakboorn. It became clear in short order that he was not going to find a book entitled *Breaking the Curse of the Seven Blades of Brakboorn.*

The blades were only mentioned in a handful of relatively recent volumes, and the information was scant. Most of it Boric already knew, and there was no mention of any sort of curse. This told him something, though: the blades had almost certainly been created after the Fall, after the library burned.

He next turned his inquiries toward Brand, the mysterious stranger who had given him the sword, but found nothing at all. As far as the Library of Avaress was concerned, there was no "Lord Brand," nor any other person of any importance named Brand in the Land of Dis. So was he someone else, traveling under an assumed name? But the witch had told him that Brand was forming a seventh kingdom beyond the Wastes of Preel—and she had used that name, Brand. So if it was an assumed name, it was one that he had stuck with for twenty years.

Boric was startled by the sound of a door opening in the next room. Looking up, he saw that the first light of dawn was filtering through the windows. He hastily grabbed up all the books on the table in front of him and retreated to a dimly lit storage room. With any luck, he could remain there undiscovered until nightfall.

He had managed to retrieve books on a great variety of topics and, having a full day to kill, he read extensively in several of them. What he found was that no matter where he started—metallurgy, history, magic—the thread eventually dead-ended in the same place: in Quanfyrr, home of the elves.

The elves, a reclusive and disagreeable people, were thought to live somewhere in the heart of the Thick Forest,[9] to the east of the Dagspaal range. No one knew exactly where, because the elves rarely left the forest and humans rarely entered it—and even more rarely exited. Xenophobic and self-sufficient, the elves almost never traded with merchants from the Six Kingdoms; their only

---

9  Named after Count Revantle Thick, whose last known words—spoken during one of the monthlong cross-country golfing campaigns that went on at the peak of the Old Realm—were, "I think my ball went in those trees over there."

known export was evil talismans. In fact, if it weren't for the occasional appearance of some accursed artifact of one kind or another, the powers that be in the Six Kingdoms might have dismissed elves as mythical creatures.

For the most part, elves are a flighty and impractical people who spend their time singing songs of a mythical golden age when elves ruled the land of Dis and reflecting on abstract philosophical questions,[10] but occasionally some mischievous elf will get it into his head to design an evil talisman of some sort—generally a ring or sword, but sometimes a more mundane object like a shovel or pair of britches. The quasi-historical ancient myths of the Old Realm relate one instance in which the Lands of Men were nearly overrun by a great army of shit trolls commanded by a peasant who had come into possession of an accursed chamber pot. The latest instance of havoc caused by someone running amok with an evil artifact of elven design,[11] occurring just before the Fall of

---

10   The question of whether animals have souls is a perennial favorite; the current prevailing view among elves is that dogs, pigs, and hedgehogs possess souls, and that cats, humans, and horses do not.

11   The Purse of Priam, which contained an endless supply of silver. The Purse of Priam caused the runaway inflation throughout the Old Realm that many historians credit as the primary impetus for the Realm's collapse. It was ultimately disposed of by Varnum the Grey, who tossed the Purse into the Cave of Infinite Regret, from which it can never be recovered. Overcome by sorrow at the loss of the Purse, Varnum spent the next twenty years scouring Dis for the Balm of Bourdain, which was said to be capable of easing any suffering. He finally found the Balm buried in a small hole not twenty feet from the Cave of Infinite Regret. Cursing the years he had wasted traveling to the remotest corners of the Realm, he squeezed some of the Balm into his mouth and waited for relief from his suffering. When nothing happened he broke into a rage, throwing the Balm of Bourdain into the Cave of Infinite Regret as well. Upon doing this he immediately noticed a small card that had been lying under the Balm that read "FOR TOPICAL USE ONLY." Varnum spent the next six months in severe gastrointestinal discomfort and then died.

the Old Realm, prompted King Calapus to send an envoy to the Thick Forest to impress upon the elves the importance of keeping better tabs on their "malevolent talismans." The elves were at first quite agreeable, swearing that no evil artifacts had been unaccounted for, promising not to create any more of them, and pledging to give the king's servants full access to the forest to see for themselves. Of course, the Thick Forest is unaccountably vast and mostly impenetrable; the king's inspectors were completely reliant on the elves to guide them to sites where evil artifacts might conceivably be stored. The elves sent the inspectors on a merry wild-goose chase through the forest that lasted nearly a year before Calapus lost patience, recalled the inspectors, and sent an army to subdue the forest. Five years later, having accomplished nothing but the decimation of his own army and the burning of several thousand acres of forestland, Calapus declared that his point had been made and withdrew his troops. A month later Calapus was beheaded by a mob in Avaress and the Old Realm fell apart.

If anyone knew how to break the curse of the Blades of Brakboorn, it was the elves. The damned elves, thought Boric. He had always hated the elves. *Everyone* hated the elves. When he was King of Ytrisk, Boric had repeatedly tried to open lines of trade with the elves to get his hands on some of their wares—like more of the rope that he had used to kill the Ogre of Chathain, which had been a gift to his father from one of the officers who had led the assault on the Thick Forest. But the elves always spurned him, insisting that they had no need of "shoddy goods that aren't designed to last a human lifetime, let alone an elven one." He'd have led an invasion of the forest himself if he hadn't been certain that it would be suicide, and a pointless suicide at that. The only thing he had returned with from that meeting was a headful of elven songs that were as catchy as they were self-aggrandizing and insipid. Even now, he could barely think of the elves without finding himself humming one of their puerile tunes. The worst of them all was the "Elven Creation Hymn," which went:

Ten thousand years ere and ten thousand years more
The spirits of Dis began their great charge
Casting leaves to the sky and dirt on the floor
A forest to make, both wondrous and large

They filled it with birds and with rocks and with plants
And with boars and with elks and with all manner of bugs
With bees and spiders and a billion or so ants
Scurrying under moss carpets and lichenous rugs

The forest, they saw, was a fine piece of work
Having trees and shrubs and plenty of deer
Devoid of all filth and all rubbish, humans and orcs
But what race can we find who deserves to live here?

Elves, elves, we are the best
Elves, elves, forget the rest
Elves, elves, casting our spells
Elves, elves, ringing our bells

And so on. It was enough to make one want to stab oneself in the head—assuming one weren't already a walking corpse.

Going to the elves meant heading deep into the mostly uncharted Thick Forest. But what other option did he have? He reflected that if the elves refused to help him, he could at least wreak some vengeance on them. Formidable as they were, the elves were unlikely to have any defenses against the undead, he thought. And even if they did, maybe he could at least manage to slaughter a few dozen of them with Brakboorn. The thought would have warmed his heart were it not an inert, rotting chunk of flesh.

When the sounds of footsteps and pages turning ceased outside the storage-room door, Boric ventured out into the library again. The building was dark. He went down to the first floor and opened the door. The streets were empty except for a stray dog who growled menacingly at him. Boric growled back and the dog ran away, whimpering.

Boric skulked down side streets and alleys, avoiding any sign of life. Most of the citizens were in bed, but lamps still burned in some houses and shops, and city watchmen patrolled the streets in pairs. He made his way to the city wall and began to climb. Scaling the wall was arduous but not impossible; the masons hadn't coated the inside of the wall with stucco as they had the outside: the wall was intended to keep barbarians out, not to keep the citizens inside. He was already halfway up the twenty-foot wall when he felt a pinprick in his lower back. Trying to focus on not losing his grip with his charred, skeletal right hand, he ignored it and continued climbing. The pinprick was followed by another, and another. Scowling, he turned to see a lone archer standing in the street some fifty feet away. He was stringing another arrow. Already three of them protruded from Boric's back.

"Can you stop that?" Boric called down to the man. "I really need to concentrate here."

The archer let loose another arrow, skewering Boric's good hand.

"Not helping," said Boric, waving his hand in a vain attempt to dislodge the arrow, the head of which protruded three inches from his palm.

"Just doing my job," said the archer, stringing another arrow. "No one's allowed to climb the wall after dark."

"So if it was daytime, I could climb to my heart's content?"

The archer thought for a moment. "No one's allowed to climb the wall. If it was daytime, you'd get a warning first." He loosed another arrow, which lodged in Boric's left thigh.

"Can you stop that for a moment?" Boric asked. "Let's think about this rationally. The wall is meant to keep people *out*, right? Barbarians and such?"

"Lot of strange rumors going around," said the man. "Talk of spies and wraiths and goblin armies. Can't take any chances." He pulled another arrow from his quiver.

Boric decided to try another tack. "Eventually you're going to run out of arrows, you know."

The archer shrugged again and strung another arrow.

"And as you can see, they aren't having much of an effect. You're just delaying the inevitable. When you run out of arrows, I'll finish climbing and be gone. And you'll be out two dozen arrows. Tell me, do you have to pay for your own arrows?"

The archer hesitated.

"Because you're not getting them back, you know. You'll lose all your arrows and have nothing to show for it. What are you going to tell your captain? That you shot all your arrows over the wall?"

"I'll tell him I was trying to stop a wraith from escaping the city."

"Why?"

"Why what?"

"Why would you want to stop a wraith from escaping the city? Correct me if I'm wrong, but don't you *want* the wraiths outside the city?"

The archer scratched his head. After a moment, he shrugged again and shot another arrow into Boric's back.

"Tell you what," said Boric. "If you stop shooting now, I'll give all your arrows back when I get to the top. But if you keep shooting, you lose all the arrows."

The archer paused to consider this. After some time he replied, "You promise you'll give them all back?"

"On the grave of...well, on my own grave, I suppose. I haven't been a wraith very long; I don't really know how the oaths work. You'll just have to trust me."

The archer shrugged again, which Boric took as agreement. He continued his climb, even slower now because of the arrow protruding from his left hand. Finally he reached the top.

"All right, give me back my arrows," called the archer.

With some difficulty, Boric worked the arrow free from his hand. The tapered head kept it from going backward; he had to pull it all the way through, leaving a pinky-sized hole in his palm. The arrow in his thigh was slightly easier. He threw them both down to the archer and began feeling around for the arrows in his back.

"Come on, then, I haven't got all night," said the archer.

"Well, you should have shot me in more accessible places!" growled Boric.

"Hello, what's all this?" he heard another voice say. A second archer had joined the first.

"Waiting for this fellow to give me back my arrows. He swore on his own grave."

"His own—"

"I'm a wraith," called Boric, trying to work an arrow out of his back. "Nice to meet you."

The second man waved to Boric. "Why don't you stop him?" he asked the first archer.

"I tried," protested the first. "Arrows don't work on the undead."

"Nonsense," said the second archer, and shot an arrow into Boric's back.

"Hey!" Boric yelled. "I'm not giving that one back!"

"See?" said the first archer. "Pointless."

"Well if that doesn't just beat all," said the second archer.

A third voice joined the discussion. "You two! What are you doing there? Why is that man on wall? Shoot him down at once!"

"No good, Captain," said the second man. "Watch." He shot another arrow into Boric's back.

"For Grovlik's sake," growled Boric. "Stop that! How do you expect me to—"

"Let me try," said the captain, taking the first man's bow. He shot an arrow into Boric's back.

"Told you," said the first archer.

"Keep shooting and I'm not giving your arrows back!" Boric shouted.

"You have to," said the first archer, sounding aggrieved. "That was the deal."

"No, the deal was that you stop shooting me and I give back the arrows you already shot. You can't keep shooting me and expect to get your arrows back."

"I didn't shoot you; they did," retorted the first archer. "I can't be held responsible for every night watchman who stumbles through here with a bow."

"It's *your bow*!" Boric growled.

"Well, now you're just nitpicking," said the man.

"Look, can we agree that it's not in anyone's interest to keep shooting arrows into my back?" asked Boric.

The men conferred among themselves and finally came to an agreement. "No more arrows," said the captain. "And you give back all the ones we've already shot."

"Fine," Boric groused, and set back to work extracting arrows. After a moment he was struck on the head with a fist-sized rock. "What in Varnoth's name was that?" Boric bellowed.

"Nobody said anything about rocks," said the second man. "Rocks are okay, right?" The other two men shrugged and nodded.

"All right, that's it," said Boric. "I take back my oath. Get your own bloody arrows." And with that, he slipped off the wall, landing with a thud on the other side. He got to his feet and began to walk south toward the Thick Forest, pulling out arrows as he went.

# Twenty

Boric reached the Thick Forest just before dawn. At the edge of the forest, the Avaressian Road turned into a narrow footpath that vanished into the woods. Boric entered the woods cautiously, following the path that he had taken years before on his mission to meet with the elves. He didn't know the exact location of Quanfyrr—no human did—but he knew roughly in which direction it lay. The expedition he had been part of years earlier had simply traveled deeper and deeper into the forest until it came upon an encampment of elves that had been erected in anticipation of humans' arrival. Boric figured if he went deep enough into the woods, the elves would find him. And if they didn't—well, he'd find Quanfyrr eventually. He had heard the legends of the strange and terrifying creatures that roamed the Thick Forest, of course, but spider-wolves, wolf-lizards, lizard-spiders, and whatever other fell beasts protected Quanfyrr held no fear for Boric. *He* was the monster here.

Monster or not, though, the Thick Forest made for tough going. Once he stepped on a mineshroom that blew most of the flesh off his left leg and twice he brushed against a red-leafed needlewort, riddling much of his upper torso with poisonous barbs. It rained for most of his first two days in the forest, drenching his wrappings. The feeling of the clammy gauze against his flesh made his spirit shiver. The worst part of the journey, though, was the three-mile-long fart marsh. Boric had never been so thankful to be on solid ground.

On the morning of his third day in the forest, Boric heard a whistling sound next to his left ear, followed by an arrow thudding into a tree in front of him.

"Oh, great," said Boric. "Arrows again." He turned to see the archer standing perhaps thirty paces away on the trail behind him: he was a slightly built man wearing an outfit of tight-fitting brown leather. His ears were slightly pointed: an elf. He had another arrow trained on Boric.

"You might as well drop the bow," said Boric. "I can't be killed. I mean, look at me." Boric was a mess: his left arm was blackened bone, his left leg looked like beef jerky, his lower body was covered with horrendous-smelling muck, and his torso was riddled with needles and arrow shafts.

The elf dipped his fingers into a pouch at his side and then touched his fingertips to the arrowhead, which was suddenly engulfed with flames. Boric shuddered. Fire and daylight were the two things he still feared.

"Fire will hurt me, it's true," said Boric, trying to maintain his composure. "But it won't kill me. And how many of those arrows do you think you can loose before I cut your throat?" Boric drew Brakslaagt and held it menacingly before him.

The elf smiled. He arched the bow and let the arrow go. Boric ducked and the arrow sailed over his right shoulder, impaling a pigeon against a pine tree. The pigeon, still alive, squawked as the flames singed its feathers. Before Boric could straighten, the elf had loosed two more arrows: one through the pigeon's head and another about six inches above it.

"Not bad," said Boric, observing the carnage. "But that last shot was a bit wide."

"The last shot wasn't aimed at the pigeon," said the elf. "It was aimed at the mosquito he was chasing."

Boric turned to look at the arrow. "Oh," he said quietly, sliding Brakslaagt back into its scabbard.

"Why have you come to our forest, stranger?" the elf asked.

"My name is Boric. I was King of Ytrisk. I have been cursed to walk Dis as a wraith because I hold this sword. It is of elven design."

The elf approached Boric, regarding his burned and tattered body. "My name is Arvin," he said. "Let me see the sword."

Boric pulled the sword slowly from the scabbard, holding it for Arvin to see. "I can't let go of it," Boric said.

Arvin nodded, studying the markings on the sword. The fuller was inscribed with a series of strange characters. Boric had assumed it was in some ancient language, but had no idea what it said.

"What does the inscription mean?" asked Boric.

"It's hard to say," said Arvin, running his fingertip along the characters.

"What do you mean? Can you read it or not?"

"Oh, I can read it, but it's hard to say. Something like *eeyauh heewahauwalalari eenyooralimeeyoi aralamaleenamaras.*"

"And that means what?"

"Hatred is the cold frog in your boot."

Boric stared at the elf. "Are you sure you have that right?"

"Oh, yes. It's hard to say in Elvish, but the meaning is quite clear. Hatred is the cold frog in your boot."

"Is that some sort of riddle?" asked Boric. "Am I supposed to solve it to break the curse?"

"Doubtful," said Arvin. "I've seen this sort of thing before. The elves design the evil artifact but leave the actual manufacturing to the dwarves. The dwarves can't read Elvish, of course, but they like to put some Elvish characters on the artifacts to give them a feel of authenticity."

"So what you're saying is that the markings are gibberish."

"Yep," said Arvin. "I mean, maybe it means something, but I wouldn't kill yourself trying to puzzle it out. No offense."

"How do I break the curse then?"

"No idea," said Arvin. "But I'm just a hunter. The council might know. Come on, I'll take you to them."

"You mean to Quanfyrr?" asked Boric, surprised. "I thought its location was a secret."

"What? Where'd you get that idea?"

"The last time I was here, many years ago, I was met at a sort of temporary encampment. I assumed it was because the location of Quanfyrr was a secret."

The elf laughed. "Boric, that *was* Quanfyrr. What, did you think we lived in some great elven metropolis in the middle of the forest? What would we build it out of, our sacred trees? And where would we get chisels and saws and hammers? We have no mines or industry, and we don't trade with anyone outside the forest. We live in tents. Quanfyrr is the Elvish word for *camp*. And there isn't just one. They're all over the place."

A light dawned in Boric's mind. "No wonder Calapus never found the elven capital," he murmured. "There *isn't* one."

"We move around all the time. Especially during wartime. You humans think in terms of battle lines and fronts, but there's no such thing in the Thick Forest. Just a bunch of random encampments. Whenever the Avaressians got close to one, we'd pick up and move. If the opportunity presented itself, we'd take out a hundred or so soldiers with arrows and then run away. You people are as loud as an ox and smell even worse, so there was never much chance the Avaressians would surprise us."

Boric shook his head in amazement. He still pretty much thought the elves were assholes, but he had to admit they were cleverer than he had given them credit for.

He followed Arvin through the woods for several miles. Occasionally Arvin would raise his bow and pin a pigeon or squirrel to a tree. Once he shot a deer.

"That's repulsive," said Boric, watching as the deer fell limp to the forest floor.

"You're one to talk," retorted Arvin.

"I just mean killing things for no good reason. Why shoot them if you're not going to eat them or use their hides or anything?"

Arvin snorted. "Tell me, Boric, how many people did you kill as King of Ytrisk?"

"Personally? A few dozen. Of course, I presided over a hundred or so executions, and if you include those killed in battle under my command—"

"And how many of them did you eat?"

"None, of course!"

"Repulsive," replied Arvin.

"That's different!" Boric growled.

"Yes," said Arvin. "I'm just killing animals."

"I meant that—"

"Yes, yes, I'm sure there was an excellent reason for every one of those deaths. I'm a hunter, Boric. That's my job. I kill things. Picking up the things I kill is a completely different job."

"Wait, so someone else follows behind you and picks up the things you kill?"

"Retriever elves," said Arvin. "Although I'm not sure they're all behind us. That first pigeon I shot is probably already in a stew."

Boric said nothing, partly because he was chagrined at his presumptuousness and partly because he was overcome with a wave of nausea at the mention of pigeon stew.

Soon they came upon a collection of scores of tents of various sizes scattered amongst the trees. An elf dropped to the ground in front of them, his foot hooked in a loop at the end of a long rope, the top of which disappeared into the leafy canopy above. He removed his foot from the rope and let go, and the loop shot back up into the trees. Boric couldn't make out the mechanics of it, but there seemed to be a system of counterweights that allowed the elves to use the ropes to easily lower themselves from high in the trees. Boric could see dozens of small platforms, rope ladders, and tents set up in and between the trees. Occasionally an elf could be seen moving from one tree to another, but for the most part the camp seemed empty.

"Welcome back, Arvin," said the elf who had dropped from above. "You're slipping. Three pigeons, four squirrels, a deer, a rabbit, and a mosquito."

"Don't forget the walking corpse," said Arvin.

The other elf regarded Boric. "It's burnt," he said.

"We can cut off the black part," said Arvin.

Boric's hand went to his sword.

"Relax," said Arvin. "I'm joking. You're completely rotten anyway. Come on, I'll take you to see the council."

The council turned out to be six elves sitting cross-legged on blankets, smoking pipes filled with something that smelled like strawberries and feet.

Arvin cleared his throat as he and Boric approached. "I found this in the woods," Arvin said, indicating Boric. "It says it's cursed by a sword of elven design."

"Greetings," said Boric. "You see —"

"Shhh!" hissed Arvin. Murmurs went up around the council. Arvin leaned close to Boric and whispered, "Corpses aren't allowed to speak in the council. Let me do the talking."

Boric wondered how often corpses had attempted to disrupt the proceedings of the council. Evidently often enough that some-one had thought to make a rule against it.

Arvin explained Boric's situation, and Boric was told to sit in the middle of the "council room" so that he and the sword could be inspected by the council members. Arvin sat next to him. The elves poked Boric with sticks and inspected his wrappings. One of the elves broke a chunk of charred flesh off Boric's elbow.

"Hey!" Boric cried, to murmurs of disapproval. Arvin glared and shook his head.

Next they passed Brakslaagt around the circle, Boric contort-ing himself to hold onto it while they twisted and turned it, handing it from one elf to another and speaking to each other in what Boric assumed was Elvish. One particularly grave-looking elf who wore his hair in long braids that went to his waist regarded the sword silently for several minutes. Finally he slid his thumb along the blade and then jerked it back, watching beads of blood appear on the tip of his thumb and roll down his wrist. "*Eeya lamareyasa weeyaramanala lasayeena*," he pronounced gravely.

"What did he say?" Boric whispered to Arvin.

Arvin whispered back, "He says, 'Don't do that; it hurts.'"

"All right, that's it," growled Boric, getting to his feet. "Do you know how to break the curse or not? Tell me now or I'll cut all your throats."

Boric became aware that he was surrounded by archers aiming fiery arrows at him. He slid Brakslaagt back into its scabbard and raised his hands. "Okay, okay. No throat-cutting. Obviously I made a mistake coming here. I'll just be on my way." He stepped away from the council and made his way to the edge of the camp. After a moment, Arvin caught up to him.

"What do you want?" Boric growled.

"You should be more patient," Arvin said. "How do you expect to learn how to break the curse if you threaten to kill anyone who can help you?"

"I won't allow my dignity to be insulted," said Boric. "And those fools have nothing to offer me."

"Boric, you've been dragging your own remains all over Dis. Just how much dignity do you think you have left? And those fools, as you call them, know more than you think. The one who cut his thumb, Caelphas? He thinks he knows one of the elves who designed the swords."

"What?" Boric cried. "He knows who designed them? I must speak to him!"

Arvin shook his head. "You should have thought of that before you threatened to cut his throat. You're not going to be allowed near any of the council members again."

Boric howled a terrible curse, frightening away all the wildlife in the area that wasn't already pinned to a tree. "Then I am doomed to walk Dis forever as a wraith!"

"Not so fast," said Arvin. "Before you stomped off, they actually said quite a bit about your sword. Some of it may be helpful to you." He began recounting the council's discussion to Boric.

Brand's mother was an elf princess who became pregnant by the seed of an Avaressian soldier during King Calapus's invasion of the Thick Forest. There was no marriage among elves and it was not uncommon for an unattached female to become pregnant. When the child was born, however, it was instantly recognized as half-human and ordered to be left to die in the forest.[12] Brand's mother couldn't bear to let the child die and left him in a basket by the side of the Avaressian Road with a note indicating that he was the half-human child of an elven princess. He was found by

---

12  Humans are thought to be a lower race by elves, and elf-human hybrids are considered to be abominations.

a traveling merchant and raised in an orphanage, where he was mercilessly teased by the other children for his slight build and pointed ears. Brand's mother was put to death for allowing the abomination to live.

Brand eventually ran away from the orphanage and disappeared for many years. One day he was found in the Thick Forest and brought before the local council. To their amazement, Brand demanded the inheritance that was due him as the son of a princess. Most of the elves wanted him thrown out of the forest, but several council members noted that Brand actually had a case: elven law, Arvin explained, was more egalitarian than human law; property and titles could be inherited both from one's mother and one's father, and there was no provision disenfranchising orphans or children of executed criminals. The law was generally thought to apply only to elves, but there was no precedent for denying an inheritance to a half-breed. A meeting of the Laocoon, or Grand Council, was called, with elves traveling from all over the Thick Forest to meet on the matter.

The Laocoon seemed headed for deadlock when Brand suggested a compromise: he would relinquish any claim to his inheritance in exchange for elven assistance with a project on which he was working. He was trying to infuse swords with a strange substance that seemed to possess magical properties. It was suspected that this is what Brand was after all along; his claim to an elven inheritance was simply a bargaining chip. The elves agreed to send three of their best craftsmen to Brand's laboratory for three years to work on the swords. The elves never returned, and it was suspected that Brand had them killed when their tenure was finished so that they could not tell anyone about what they had been working on. When reports surfaced that several human kings were carrying swords that appeared to be of elven design, the elves suspected that it was the work of Brand. The exact nature of the swords remained unknown; the elves hadn't known anything about a curse until Boric showed up.

"Well that's just fantastic," said Boric. "So nobody knows anything about the curse."

"No," said Arvin. "But here's the thing: we elves try to keep to ourselves. We don't like a lot of attention. I know you humans must think that we're constantly sending out evil artifacts to wreak havoc in the Six Kingdoms, but frankly it's bad publicity for us. Do you think we like being invaded by human armies?"

"What's your point?" asked Boric.

"My point is that if there's any way we can contain the damage caused by these swords, we'll do it. We just don't have much to go on right now. My suggestion would be to try to get your hands on some of this substance that Brand used to create the swords. Bring it back here and our alchemists may be able to determine the nature of its hold over you."

"Where would I get any of this substance? I don't have any idea what it is."

"It's some sort of mineral, or metal," said Arvin. "When Brand came to the Thick Forest, he came from the north. There's no reason for anyone to come from the north, even if they were traveling from the Wastes of Preel. It would be much simpler to travel south through Avaress. And Caelphas says he had the red dust of the Feldspaal Mountains on his boots."

"That's dwarven territory," said Boric.

"Exactly," said Arvin. "My guess is that the substance Brand used in the swords was unearthed by the dwarves in the mines of Feldspaal. If you go there, you may be able to find the mine where the substance was found. Get some of it and return here. The council will do what it can for you."

"Ugh," said Boric.

"The council isn't so bad," said Arvin.

"No, it's not that," said Boric.

"What then?"

"More walking," Boric muttered, shaking his head.

# Twenty-One

Arvin convinced Boric to allow the elven healers to make some repairs to his body before he left for the Feldspaal Mountains. After an hour of deliberations, however, the healers threw up their hands and walked off, leaving the job to the taxidermy elves, who did a remarkable job of making Boric look almost human again. His missing flesh was replaced with pouches of sawdust and his torn and filthy wrappings were swapped for fresh gauze. They even wrapped the lower part of his face with a scarf and replaced his tattered cloak. He looked like a shiftless brigand when they were done, but this was a vast improvement over mutilated corpse. There followed an awkward moment during which several of the taxidermists, who had misunderstood the purpose of their endeavor, insisted they be allowed to place their creation in a diorama with three stuffed wolves and a glass waterfall. They were more than a bit put out when their masterpiece stomped off into the woods.

Three days later—after managing to avoid the mineshrooms and red-leafed needleworts (but not a razor fern that sliced half-way through his right arm), Boric found himself at the foot of the Dagspaal Mountains. They were gigantic—not only thousands of feet high, but extending as far as he could see in every direction except the one from which he had come. There could be hundreds of mines in these mountains; finding the source of Brand's mysterious substance could take years. The utter hopelessness of his task struck him anew.

Fighting against the urge to find a cave in which to once again lie down and give up, he forced himself to think rationally. He knew that the dwarves lived primarily to the north and east, so the mine he was looking for was probably in that direction. He decided to head north along the edge of the Feldspaals, looking for any sign of the reddish dust that had been on Brand's boots. It was the only lead he had.

Just before dawn, he caught sight of something in the sky that he at first thought was a very large bird. But it was soon apparent that it was much larger than even the largest bird he had ever seen. With a great gust of wind, Bubbles the wyndbahr landed right in front of him.

"Has it been a week already?" he asked.

"Yep," said Viriana, dismounting Bubbles. "No luck with the curse yet, huh?"

"Bloody elves sent me up here," replied Boric. "I have to find the mine where they got the stuff that they used to make the sword."

"Are you sure they weren't just trying to get rid of you?"

"I have no idea," said Boric. "Probably. I'm never going to find it. Hey, you haven't seen any mines around here, have you? Preferably some place where the dirt is red?"

Viriana shook her head. "Doesn't ring any bells. But hey, there's something kind of weird a few miles north of here. Hop on and I'll take you there."

Boric paused, looking toward the lightening sky in the east. He really needed to find a place to hunker down for the day. On the other hand, getting a ride with Viriana would save him several miles of walking. And maybe he'd be able to spot the mine from up above.

"Now or never," said the Eytrith. "I have a schedule to keep."

"Okay," said Boric, hopping onto the wyndbahr's back. Bubbles launched into the air.

Boric couldn't see anything noteworthy in the mountains, but after a minute or so he saw what Viriana was talking about: two parallel lines running east-west across the Wastes of Preel. The lines ran as far as he could see to the east and disappeared into a tunnel in the mountainside to the west. Bubbles landed just to the south of them and Boric jumped off to inspect the lines more closely. The lines were in fact a pair of thick metal rails, spaced about four feet apart, secured to a series of perpendicular wooden ties. The spaces between the ties were filled with gravel. Boric knew that the dwarves sometimes used carts on a system of rails to move dirt and ore from their mines, but he had never heard of a rail system anywhere near as large as this. There was only one possible terminus for a railway across the Wastes of Preel: the stronghold of "Lord Brand." But what was transported on the rails?

"Gotta go," said Viriana. "I can leave you here or take you back to the forest."

Boric hesitated again. Any second the sun would peek above the horizon. If he stayed here, the tunnel was the only place to hide. But if he had Viriana take him back to the forest, that meant at least another ten miles of walking. He was *so* sick of walking.

"I think I'm good," said Boric.

"Okay, then," said Viriana. "In that case, I shall return in one week! Pray that you have broken the curse by then!"

"Yeah, yeah," said Boric.

"No, seriously. I can't keep coming back for you. You've got one week, that's it."

"And if I don't break the enchantment by then?"

Viriana shrugged. "Just do it, okay?" She dug her heels into Bubbles and the wyndbahr leapt into the air.

Boric ran along the rails toward the tunnel. Peering inside, he could see that the rails disappeared around a corner perhaps a quarter mile in. The tunnel was only slightly wider than the rails and barely tall enough for Boric to stand. There was no way of knowing how long it was. But he had no choice: already the first rays of the sun were burning his back. He stepped into the tunnel.

The air in the tunnel was cool and still, and Boric found the near-total darkness comforting. He rounded the corner to see that the tracks extended perhaps another quarter mile to an opening on the far side. His next move was unclear. He couldn't exit the tunnel during the day, but he feared the possibility that a cart would come through while he was in the tunnel. Even if he didn't get run over, he was certain to be caught skulking in the tunnel. He had no quarrel with the dwarves and he would prefer not to get into a fight with them if he could avoid it. There might come a time when he would need their help, and he'd prefer that their first meeting not be in a dark tunnel where he would probably scare them half to death.

He managed to find a crevice in the tunnel where he could hide and not be in the way of a passing cart. With any luck, he wouldn't be noticed. He had no idea how often the rails were used—or even *if* they were used, but he preferred not to wait on the tracks if he could avoid it.

As it turned out, he didn't have to wait long. Within an hour he heard a rumbling on the tracks that indicated a something was approaching. Seeing nothing to the west, he ventured a look around the corner and saw, in the distance, what looked like a mule approaching. As it got closer, he saw that it was actually several mules traveling in single-file along the tracks. He ducked back into his crevice and waited for the procession to pass.

It took a while. As slow as the mules had been traveling, they slowed down even more in the tunnel, as it was barely large enough for them to fit through. Boric reminded himself that the tunnel was almost pitch black; the mules had to be navigating entirely by the feel of the rails against their hooves. They brayed and snorted nervously. "Come on, ya lazy brutes!" growled a gruff voice. "Ya been through this tunnel a hundred times. We'll never make it to Buren-Gandt before nightfall at this rate!" Boric wondered if the animals could sense that something wasn't right. There was the sound of a whip cracking and more piteous braying. At long last, the first of the mules approached Boric's hiding place. It stubbornly refused to go any farther.

"Yer halfway through now, stupid!" growled the voice. "Keep movin'!" The whip cracked again and the mule jerked forward. It raised its muzzle in the air and opened its mouth in a sort of grimace, as if smelling something rotten. It slowly turned its head to face Boric, who was as still as a corpse. There was no way the animal could see him, but it seemed to sense that something was lurking in the dark. Its eyes and nostrils went wide and it broke into a run. The mules behind it were pulled forward and each of them panicked in turn as it reached Boric. Boric counted seven of them. The whole team was now running at top speed. Behind them, a short, solidly built man with a long brown beard sat in a cart pulling on the reins. "Slow down, ya idiot mules! Yer gonna break yer legs!" But the mules kept running.

Behind the driver's cart followed a series of a dozen or so mostly empty carts. Boric saw that several of them contained tarps that could be used to cover cargo. As the last one passed, Boric stepped out of the crevice and caught hold of it, vaulting into the cart. He grabbed a tarp and did his best to tie it to the hooks on the corners of the cart. As the train emerged into the sunlight, he ducked under the tarp and pulled his cloak tightly around him. The mules seemed reassured by the open air and slowed to a walk. It wasn't a very dignified way to travel, but it beat walking—and it seemed his best bet to find the mine he was looking for. The only explanation for such an extensive rail system was the need to move large amounts of something very valuable from the Feldspaal Mountains to Brand's stronghold.

The driver had mentioned "getting to Buren-Gandt before nightfall." Boric had never heard of such a place, but he assumed it was the location of the mine. He could only hope that the driver's estimate of his arrival time was roughly accurate—and that there weren't any other stops along the way. He listened intently for any sign that the train was slowing or approaching any sort of settlement or outpost, but he heard nothing but the rhythmic clomping of hooves on the gravel and the occasional squeak of a metal wheel on the rails. For several hours they seemed to be on a slight upward slope that gradually grew steeper. Then they reached a long downhill grade.

He smelled Buren-Gandt before he heard it: the scent of burning coal filled the air. Venturing a glance from under the tarp, he saw that the sky was dark with soot. There was no sign of any sort of settlement yet, but it had to be close. The sun had disappeared behind the mountains and the light was growing dim. Boric climbed out of the cart and dropped onto the tracks, shielding his eyes from the remaining daylight.

He was in a valley in the middle of the Feldspaal Mountains, with great snowy peaks towering on all sides. Boric continued along the track, following the mule train at a hundred paces or so. He doubted the driver would look back, and in any case would be unlikely to make him out in the dying light. The smoke grew thicker and echoes of clanging machinery filled the valley. Soon the track began a precipitous drop; the mules were no longer pulling the train so much as breaking its descent. Here the track was sunk in an ever-deepening crevice carved into the rock, and he could see that ahead the valley fell away into a vast canyon with sheer rock sides. The track disappeared around a corner to the left and Boric could see that it continued on the other side of the canyon, spiraling ever downward. Rather than follow the train down through the crevice, Boric remained at the top of the canyon, creeping stealthily toward the rim. He noticed that the dust clinging to his boots was red. Reaching the edge, he peered over into the chasm below.

The sight filled him with awe. The canyon was probably a mile deep at its deepest, roughly circular and maybe a mile wide; it had been excavated to varying depths in different places and each level swarmed with dwarves. Some were swinging picks; others were digging with shovels; still others were moving piles of rock with wheelbarrows. In the middle of it all, about a half a mile down, sat a giant metal machine that was unlike anything Boric had ever seen. There was a great revolving wheel some fifty feet high, and next to it a huge cantilevered metal beam that rocked up and down like a giant hammering a nail. Alongside this was a riveted iron tank the size of one of the Kra'al Brobdingdon's massive guard towers. Below the tank was a gigantic furnace that blazed with such intense heat that Boric could feel it at the canyon's rim, and with such light that it illuminated the entire canyon almost as if it were day.

Four metal chutes ran to the furnace, each chute manned by a score of dwarves, who were frantically shoveling coal into them. At the same time, other groups of dwarves were delivering wheelbarrow loads of coal to keep the dwarves on the chutes supplied. A third set of dwarves rested out of the way of the commotion, drinking and dousing themselves with water from a trough. Every so often a group of the resting dwarves would take the place of the coal-delivering dwarves, the coal-delivering dwarves would take the place of the chute-filling dwarves, and the chute-filling dwarves would head to the resting area. No whistle or bell sounded, but somehow the dwarves all knew exactly where they were supposed to be and when they were supposed to switch places. After some time, Boric realized that they were all working in time with the movements of the giant beam. Every switch was ten beats apart, and the schedules of the workers at each of the four chutes were staggered by ten beats. The shrewdness of this system was instantly evident: the workers shoveling coal were always fresh, so they could keep the furnace roaring at full capacity; none of the workers ever got in each other's way; and everyone knew what they were supposed to be doing at all times. It was still unclear what the machine actually did, of course, other than cast a hellish glow over the canyon, belch foul smoke into the air, and throw off nearly as much heat as the midday sun, but Boric was convinced that whoever had designed this scheme—not to mention the machine itself—was some kind of diabolical genius. Brand, he thought. It had to be.

He was still trying to figure out what Brand was trying to accomplish with his infernal machine when he was gripped by both arms and thrown into the canyon.

Boric stared at his own body lying broken on the canyon floor. Two figures in black stood over him, growling, hissing, and poking at his corpse. Boric wanted nothing more than to float away, to leave his wretched carcass and this accursed place, but there was no denying the inexorable pull of Brakslaagt. No matter how hard he fought, he couldn't get away, and suddenly it wasn't some inert hunk of flesh the wraiths were kicking and poking; it was Boric.

"Hey!" he yelled. "Cut that out!"

"You see," said one of the wraiths. "He is like us. The Master summoned him, and he came."

"No one summoned me," growled Boric, getting to his feet. "I am here to learn the secret of the curse of the Seven Blades of Brakslaagt. So that I can be free. So that we can all be free."

"Are you?" said a voice behind him. Boric spun to see another man approaching. He was tall—certainly not a dwarf, and he looked to be quite young. He was dressed in a simple tunic with no visible sign of rank but somehow managed to convey an unquestionable air of authority. His complexion was fair and the glow of the furnace gave his hair and face a hellish sheen.

"And who might you be, lad?" challenged Boric. "Some eager young sycophant of His Insolence Lord Brand?" The wraiths moved closer to Boric, gripping his arms tightly.

The young man smiled. "His son, actually," he replied. "My name is Leto. I run the mining operation here."

"His…" Boric started. Could this really be Brand's son? He didn't really look that much like Brand, but it was difficult to tell in the harsh red light. Half of his face glowed like crimson and the other half was in shadow.

"Now, Boric, is it?" said the young man. "Why don't you tell me about this curse you're so desperate to break."

"Don't toy with me, lad," growled Boric. "You know full well the curse I speak of. These other good men and I have been cursed to walk Dis as dead men."

"Really?" asked Leto. "Gentlemen, is this true? Have you been cursed?"

"No, m'lord," said the wraiths in unison. The one to Boric's left added, "We wish only to serve Lord Brand."

"OK, well they're pretty far gone," said Boric. "But I still remember what it was like to be human, and I don't appreciate being jerked around like a puppet."

Leto laughed. "No, I suppose you wouldn't," he said. "You spent your life treating others as puppets, and now that it's your turn, you chafe at the wires. Tell me, Boric, what would you do if you were free?"

"I'd leave this petty world and go to my reward in the Hall of Avandoor," said Boric.

"Oh, the Hall of Avandoor!" cried Leto. "And what will you do there? Boast about the ogre you slew and the trolls you minced?"

"Well, yes," replied Boric. "And you know, eat mutton and drink mead, that sort of thing."

"And tell me, oh Boric the Implacable, just how do you think you rate amongst the giant-killers and dragon-slayers?"

"I don't have, like, an exact number, if that's what you're looking for," said Boric. Yes I do, he thought: eighty-seven.

"Still, wouldn't you like an opportunity to bump your score up a bit, as it were? Kill another bugbear or two?"

Boric shook his head. "It doesn't count because I'm already dead. Besides, I'm not sure bugbears are worth much."

Leto stared at him. "Do you even listen to yourself when you talk?"

"What?" Boric asked. "I'm just saying, they don't count it as a slaying if you're dead. Frankly, the rules are pretty arbitrary. I'm totally getting shafted out of an ogre slaying *and* a dragon slaying."

Leto shook his head. "Wow. My mother was right about you. I thought she was exaggerating, but she was totally right, as usual. Tie him up and throw him on the next train to Brandsveid. I'm done with him." Leto turned and began walking away.

"As you wish, m'lord," said the wraiths, gripping Boric's arms tightly.

"Wait, your mother?" asked Boric. "Who's your mother?"

"I believe you met her once," said Leto, stopping to face Boric. "Her name is Milah."

# Twenty-Two

Boric spent the next three days tied up in a cart bound for Brand's stronghold. The journey was uneventful; the Wastes of Preel consisted of nothing but hundreds of miles of salty muck. Legend held that the Wastes had once been a sea. There were no settlements and no animal or plant life to speak of. It was difficult to traverse by foot, and even if Boric could have worked his way out of the ropes, the two wraiths were traveling with him to prevent his escape. He was going to meet Brand, whether he was ready for him or not.

Was it true that Leto was Milah's son by Brand? And was Milah with Brand now? The thought made him feel sick. How could she do that to him? Didn't she realize what Brand had done to him? Or had she been in league with him all along? It did seem a little suspicious that he met Milah only two days after meeting Brand. But what had she been angling for? What did her magic mirrors have to do with Brand and the Blades of Brakboorn? Clearly he was missing something, but what? And who did Leto think he was, anyway? What was he getting at with his dismissive talk about Boric's curse? It figured that a pretentious upstart like "Lord Brand" would sire an uppity brat like Leto. Boric planned to kill both of them at the first opportunity. Well, after figuring out how to break his curse, of course.

Twice the train stopped and made camp. No one bothered to check on Boric, and why would they? Presumably he was still dead. Occasionally, for shorter intervals, the train would stop so the driver could water the mules. During some of these stops, Boric heard voices and what sounded like another train passing. He couldn't make any sense of this: there was only one set of tracks. It was possible, of course, that there were side rails that the driver could direct the train onto, but how would he know when to pull over? Even if the drivers used a flag system like that used by the signalmen in the army of Ytrisk, flags could only be seen at a distance of a few miles. Unless there were side rails every couple of miles, the trains would constantly be backtracking to get out of each other's way. But the passing occurred without incident every single time. Could it be that the schedule of the trains was kept as precisely as that of the dwarves in Buren-Gandt? It seemed impossible. There was no giant hammer here to help them keep time, and how could any such system account for unexpected contingencies like bad weather or a mule with a broken leg? It made no sense.

Nor could Boric figure out why Brand needed such a gigantic mining operation. Assuming the mine at Buren-Gandt was the source of the material used in the swords, what could he possibly need such a vast amount for? Was he making swords to enslave every man in Dis? The possibility filled him with sudden dread. Of course. He recalled the swords of simple but excellent workmanship that half the nobles in Ytrisk were using—the same sort of sword used by Clovis the Technical Dragon-Slayer. Having enslaved the former kings of the Six Kingdoms, Boric had moved on to the dukes and counts. When they died, he would have a wraith army composed of the greatest swordsmen and tacticians in Dis—men who knew the defenses of every castle in the land. There would be no stopping him. The fact that Clovis hadn't turned into a wraith militated against this line of reasoning, but maybe his sword had been defective. There was no other explanation: Brand intended to enslave all of Dis. All the more reason for Boric to kill him.

On the evening of the third day, the train finally stopped amongst the sound of the clanking of metal and men shouting in a strange, harsh-sounding language. The tarp on his cart was removed and he was hauled out and thrown on the ground by the wraiths. They cut his ropes and pulled him to his feet.

Boric was once again on the floor of a valley surrounded by mountain peaks. But this place had a more desolate, barren feel than Buren-Gandt. Rather than reddish-brown, the ground was as gray as ash, and the peaks were jagged and treeless. In fact, no trees or other plant life could be seen.

The wraiths gripped Boric's arms and spun him around, dragging him toward a massive edifice built into a near-vertical cliff wall. It was easily double the size of Kra'al Brobdingdon, with towers that rivaled Avaressa's tallest buildings. In front of the castle was the source of all the commotion: a goblin army, easily ten thousand strong, broken into regiments that were marching in formation around the vast and barren valley floor. Was this the army that Brand intended to use to conquer the Six Kingdoms? If so, he wasn't as smart as Boric had thought: goblins were unruly and undisciplined, excelling only at hit-and-runs and other guerilla tactics. Marching a goblin army across the Wastes of Preel would be like trying to push a chess set across a sandbox.

The wraiths ushered Boric through the marching ground and across a drawbridge that was lowered over the semicircular moat barring access to the front of the castle. Looking down, Boric saw that the moat was actually a chasm in the rock. It appeared to be hundreds of feet deep. Brand had picked the location for his castle well: anyone falling down there wouldn't be getting up again. Once across the drawbridge, they entered the castle and walked through a long hall lined with goblin guards wearing plate armor and bearing halberds. Reaching the end of the hall, one of the guards pulled aside a sliding metal gate and shoved Boric into a small, square, windowless room. The wraiths followed closely behind.

"Top floor," said one of the wraiths.

"Huh?" said Boric. He turned to see a small goblin standing in the corner of the room. He leaned into a horn-like device protruding from the wall of the room and shouted, "TOP FLOOR, STAN!"

There was a sound of grunting and the pulling of chains and the whole room jerked upward a few inches, nearly causing Boric to lose his balance. After the initial jolt the room moved more smoothly, and if it weren't for the sight of floors passing behind the metal gate and the clinking of chains, he might not have even known they were moving. The other wraiths and the goblin seemed to find the situation perfectly normal, so Boric decided not to make a fool of himself by exclaiming about the strange moving room. It was an ingenious invention, he thought; many times he had wished for some sort of magical device to transport him to the top of the eighty-foot guard towers of Kra'al Brobdingdon. Presumably the moving room was a variation on the sort of hoist used by builders to move materials to the upper levels of scaffolds, but he had never heard of such a thing being constructed inside a building— or being used to move people.

At last the room stopped at what Boric assumed was the top level of the castle. The wraiths prodded Boric forward, following close behind him. The goblin attendant remained behind in the movable room, closing the gate behind them. The three wraiths strode through a long, narrow hall, stopping at the end to knock on a heavy wooden door. From within, a soft voice said, "Come."

The wraiths opened the door. A breathtakingly beautiful woman in a green dress stood just inside. The slightest hints of wrinkles were visible at the corners of her mouth, and her long red hair was streaked with gray. "Leave us," she said to the two wraiths. Boric stepped inside and she closed the door behind him.

"Milah," said Boric. "You look beautiful. Just as you did twenty years ago."

"Thank you, Boric," said Milah. "I wish I could say the same about you."

"In fairness, I've been dead for over two weeks."

"Yes, I heard," said Milah. "I'm so sorry about that."

"You're *sorry*? Milah, your beloved Brand did this to me. How could you betray me this way?"

"How could *I* betray *you*?" asked Milah with a laugh. "Boric, you denied knowing me. You let me make a fool of myself. You left me alone in Brobdingdon with nothing!"

"I saved your life!" Boric spat. "And I gave you all the money I had on me. What would you have me do, Milah? Try to sell my father on your crazy mirror scheme? On my wedding day?"

"Yes!" screamed Milah. "Yes, that's *exactly* what I expected you to do. Of course at the time I was under the impression that you were a decent human being."

"Ha!" cried Boric. "This from the woman who is sleeping with Brand, the man who plots to conquer all of Dis with an army of the undead!"

Milah shot Boric a puzzled look, then burst into laughter. "That's what you think Brand is up to? Conquering the Six Kingdoms with an army of wraiths? What would be the point of *that*?"

Boric was taken aback by this response. "What do you mean? The point would be to, you know, conquer all of Dis and rule it with an iron fist."

"But what kind of world would that be?" asked Milah. "Mass killing, thousands in slavery, and walking corpses running rampant across the land? Do you think Brand is some sort of monster?"

"Of *course* he's a monster!" Boric cried, baffled at Milah's denseness. "Have you not seen the goblin army he's assembled outside?"

Milah's hand went to her forehead. "Oh, Boric. Poor, silly, deluded Boric."

"Mock me if you wish, woman," growled Boric, "but your lover Brand is a madman bent on conquest. Beware the day your beauty fades, woman, because Brand will cast you aside the moment you are no longer of use to him."

Milah raised her hand as if to slap Boric, but thought better of it. "You wouldn't even feel it, would you?" she said. "You feel no pain, much less shame. Any humanity that you once had is rapidly slipping away. You aren't yourself. And for that reason, I forgive you your insult. I wish your mother had the comfort of knowing you weren't in your right mind."

Boric was now even more baffled. Milah was making no sense at all. "My mother?" he asked. "My mother has been dead for eight years. And I never showed her anything but respect."

Milah burst into laughter again, then stopped abruptly. "By Varnoth," she gasped. "You don't know, do you? You really don't know."

"What in Dis are you talking about, Milah? Don't know what?"

"Did you never wonder why you don't look like either of your brothers? Why they were such ugly, bumbling dolts, and you... were not? Or, for that matter, why the Witch of Twyllic happened to be found guilty of practicing 'dark magic' just days after you were born?"

Boric's mind reeled. "But that's not...how could they have..."

"Gulbayna and the Witch...that is, Anna, were pregnant at the same time. Anna was the head midwife at Kra'al Brobdingdon at the time. Gulbayna's baby was stillborn, and she blamed Anna. Two days later, Anna gave birth to a strapping, ten-pound baby that uncannily resembled your father, King Toric. Gulbayna's baby was buried quietly and Anna was brought up on charges of using dark magic. She was given the choice of being exiled and giving up the baby or being burned alive with her son in her arms. She chose exile. Everyone in Ytrisk knows the rumors, Boric. Well, everyone but you, apparently. I'm sorry to have to tell you this way."

Boric stood in silent shock. What Milah said made perfect sense. How had he not figured this out sooner? Had he just not wanted to know?

"I'm sorry, Boric," said Milah. "I really thought you knew. And I'm sorry for thinking you were a monster all these years. Despite the way you treated me, I don't think you're a monster. You're just really, really dense. You probably actually thought you were protecting me by disavowing any knowledge of me or the mirrors."

Boric raised his hands in supplication. "Of course I was," he protested weakly, still trying to come to terms with what she had told him. "If I'd have let my father set you up with a laboratory with money from the royal treasury and you failed…"

"Ah, there's the Boric I know," said Milah. "Condescending even in defeat. Didn't I tell you once that you talk too much? Come with me, Boric. I want to show you something."

# Twenty-Three

Boric stood with Milah on a scaffold overlooking a cavernous room beneath Kra'al Brandskelt. Below them, hundreds of workers toiled at workbenches and operated large, strange-looking machines. The room was hot and stuffy and filled with the clanging of tools and machines. But the most startling thing was the workers themselves: they were of virtually every race in Dis. There were elves, dwarves, humans, and goblins, all working side by side. Boric was amazed to see that some of the larger machines were actually operated by ogres, who seemed perfectly content to use their brute strength to pull levers or turn wheels rather than tear people limb from limb. Boric never would have believed it if he hadn't seen it with his own eyes—or what was left of his eyes, anyway.

"How do you…" Boric started.

"How do we what?"

"How do you keep them from killing each other?"

Milah shook her head, smiling. "Why would they kill each other? This is a cooperative enterprise. They all need each other to get the work done. And they're paid on a piece rate, so the more work they do, the more they get paid. This may surprise you, Boric, but there are ways of dealing with problems besides killing things. Even the ogres understand that."

Boric stared silently out at the workroom for some time. He couldn't begin to make sense of the complex operations taking place down there. Finally, he said, "So what are they making? Weapons?"

Milah laughed. "No, Boric. They're making mirrors. Like the kind that I showed you twenty years ago, but much improved."

"But why? What do you need so many mirrors for?"

"All sorts of things," Milah replied. "Communicating with Leto at the Buren-Gandt, signaling commands to the goblin army units, coordinating the trains...But we sell most of them. We've sold dozens of them to kings of the Six Kingdoms and other noblemen. I don't think we've sold any in Ytrisk yet, because it's so far away, but I'm sure we soon will. Merchants use them for communicating orders to their suppliers and taking orders from customers. In fact, the merchant class is our biggest customer base. They're starting to resell the mirrors at a profit."

"What? How can you let them do that? They're pocketing money that rightly belongs to you!"

"We don't mind," said Milah. "The merchants can go places we can't. What is it to us if they mark up the price a bit? The customer gets what they want, we get what we want, and the merchants make a little money off the deal. What you fail to understand, Boric, is that life doesn't have to be all about killing people and taking their stuff. These mirrors have the potential to make Dis a better place."

"How's that?"

"They can help us communicate with each other. More communication means less misunderstanding. And just imagine what could happen if a Quirini merchant could instantly know what an Ytriskian customer wants? Whole new routes of trade will open up. Everyone will be doing business with everyone else, all across Dis. The Six Kingdoms will be united in a way they never were under the Old Realm."

"And if that fails, there's always the goblin army, right?" said Boric.

Milah sighed. "Boric, this entire area is overrun with goblins. You know what they were doing before Brand arrived? Killing each other and occasionally sending raiding parties out to murder travelers on the road to Quirin. We put as many of them to work in the castle as we can, but we just don't have enough zelaznium ore to keep them all busy making mirrors. So yes, we have a few thousand goblins marching around in front of the castle. What else are we going to do with them?"

"Brand is clever, I'll give him that," said Boric. "He seems to have thought of everything."

Milah shook her head. "The goblin army wasn't Brand's idea. He wanted to exterminate them. It was Leto who thought of putting them to work. Leto organized the workroom as well. And I guess you saw his operation at Burn-Gandt. Impressive, isn't it?"

"More like terrifying," replied Boric. "Dwarves crawling all over in the hellish glow from that furnace...what is that infernal machine anyway?"

"One of Leto's inventions," Milah said proudly. "You see, the dwarves dug too deep in the mountains—"

"I knew it!" cried Boric. "They released some unspeakable evil from deep inside of Dis, didn't they? That machine is the only thing containing it. I'm telling you, Milah, I could feel the evil pouring out of that thing."

Milah laughed. "Don't be ridiculous, Boric. There's no evil in it. It's just a machine. Leto calls it a steam engine. You see, the dwarves dug below the water table and the mines kept flooding. They had been using hand pumps to pull the water out, but they aren't practical on a large scale. Leto had read about an alchemist who had experimented with a spinning wheel that was powered by steam. You put the water in a tank and heat it, and the escaping steam makes the wheel spin. He applied that principle to a water pump, first on a small scale, and then on a much bigger scale at Buren-Gandt. Right now he's experimenting with trying to make an engine that's small enough and light enough to fit on a rail car. He thinks eventually we'll be able to replace mules with steam engines that can run all day and night. Can you imagine?"

"It sounds awful," said Boric. "And what's wrong with mules anyway?"

"There's nothing *wrong* with them," said Milah. "But they do need to eat and sleep, and they can be a bit ornery. And of course they're difficult to breed, because, well, being of two different species—"

"What my lovely wife is trying to tell you, Boric, is that mules are half-breeds."

Boric turned to see a man walking toward them on the scaffold. Brand. He looked the same as he did twenty years earlier. Boric drew his sword and advanced.

"Boric, stop!" cried Milah.

But Boric could think only of his curse—of what Brand had taken from him, and the monster Boric had become.

"Tell me how to break the curse, Brand, or die where you stand!" Immediately regretting this couplet, Boric tried again. "Tell me the secret or die!"

Brand drew his own sword. It was identical to Brakslaagt, but without the Elvish markings. "There is no secret!" Brand protested. "Or if there is, I don't know it. I never meant for you to turn into a wraith, Boric. It was an accident!"

Boric fell upon Brand, swinging his sword at Brand's side. Brand parried. "An accident!" Boric cried. "It was an accident that you gave me a cursed sword?"

"I didn't know about the curse," insisted Brand, parrying another blow. "Those seven blades were an experiment. The elves were still trying to figure out how to control the power of the mineral. Obviously something went wrong."

Boric sliced from the right and then feinted left, throwing Brand off balance. Brand was a decent swordsman, but no match for Boric. Boric wedged his blade between Brand's cross-guard and blade and twisted. Brand's sword fell to the scaffold. Boric took a step forward and raised his blade to Brand's throat. "You lie," Boric hissed.

"Please, Boric," said Milah, behind him. "He's telling the truth. Zelaznium is very tricky to work with."

"Zelaznium?" Boric asked, trying to remember where he had heard the word. "The stuff the mirrors are made of? Why would you put that in swords?"

"Because the swords serve the same purpose," said Milah.

"Nonsense," said Boric, pressing the tip of Brakslaagt against Brand's throat. A trickle of blood ran to Brand's collarbone. "Tell me how to break the enchantment!"

"It's the truth, Boric," gasped Brand. "I don't know any more about the curse than you do. When the first wraith showed up here ten years ago, he frightened me nearly to death. That was King Loren of Avaress. He had been run out of a dozen towns and finally came here because he had no place else to go. They kept coming every few years after that. I try to keep them busy, bossing the goblins around and whatnot, but it's not an easy existence, being a wraith. They were ecstatic when I sent them to chase after you. I hope they weren't too aggressive."

"Liar!" howled Boric. "You bribed Captain Randor to kill me!"

"What? No! Why would I do that?"

"To turn me into a wraith, of course."

"Twenty years after giving you Brakslaagt? If I'd wanted you dead, you'd have died long ago, Boric."

Boric pulled the sword back just a hair. "Then who had me killed?"

"My best guess is that it was your brother, Yoric."

"Yoric is dead!"

"Apparently not. He reappeared shortly after your death, leading a ragtag band of Vorgals into Brobdingdon. Evidently he faked his death on Bjill. He produced a will that indicated you had selected him as your heir. It was widely believed to be forged, but no one dared oppose him for fear that the Vorgals would lay waste to the city. And that clubfooted nitwit you had placed on the throne didn't exactly rally a lot of popular support. Yoric is now King of Ytrisk. I understand he even married your widow, Urgulana, to help secure his claim."

"Lies!" cried Boric, pressing the sword again to Brand's throat. Brand's whole story was preposterous, particularly the part about Yoric willingly marrying that beast Urgulana. "This is your last chance. Tell me how to break the curse or die!"

"Boric, please," pleaded Milah. "Don't kill him. If not for my sake, then for Leto's."

This gave Boric pause. He was having trouble keeping up with the number of bizarre nonsequiturs in this exchange. "Leto? What does your son have to do with any of this?"

"It's what I was trying to tell you before you attacked me," Brand said. "I'm a half-breed. Like a mule. Half-human and half-elf. As a result, I'm sterile. I can't have children of my own."

"But then how…?" Boric began.

"I was already pregnant when I met Brand," said Milah. "Brand is the only father he has ever known, but we've never withheld the truth from Leto. He's your son, Boric."

Boric stumbled backward, bracing himself against the railing of the scaffold. His meeting with Brand was not turning out at all the way he had planned. If he could have dropped his sword, he would have. "Is this…are there any more familial revelations you'd care to make, Milah?"

"I think that's pretty much it," said Milah, rubbing her chin with her thumb and forefinger. "Leto is your son, the Witch of Twyllic is your mother, and your brother Yoric is King of Ytrisk. That about covers it." Boric looked at Brand, who nodded. Brand was mopping the blood from his throat with his handkerchief.

"He's the best of both of us, Boric," Milah said. "He's brave and clever and handsome like you, and he has my genius for inventing things. And with Brand's influence, he has become a master of administration and organization. Very soon, in fact, I think he's going to begin chafing at Brand's control over him. I wouldn't be surprised if he sets off on some enterprise of his own. You should be very proud."

Proud? thought Boric. Of a son I never knew I had? He reflected that Leto had known when they met that Boric was his true father. And yet he spoke condescendingly, even dismissively to Boric. Not to mention that he had Boric tied up and thrown in a cart for three days. What had Boric done to deserve such treatment? Another question nagged at him as well: "What did you mean that the swords serve the same purpose as the mirrors?"

"Long-range communication," answered Brand. "It might help if I start at the beginning."

# Twenty-Four

Shortly after Brand was left on the side of the Avaressian Road by his mother, a traveling merchant found him and brought him to an orphanage in Avaressa. He was badly treated at the orphanage and ran away when he was fourteen, living as a pickpocket on the streets of Avaressa. One day he lifted a small bag of silvery dust from an emissary of the court who had just returned from a summit with the dwarves to the north. Brand was fascinated by the substance: it was finer and lighter than silver and possessed some very strange properties. He noticed, for instance, that he could separate the dust into two piles and then form the first pile into some figure, such as a circle, and the second pile would mimic the first. Even if he put a box over the second pile, when he lifted the box he would see that the pile had formed the same shape as the first. Suspecting that some sort of magic was at work, Brand brought the dust to a local alchemist, telling him he could keep the dust if he could tell Brand where it had come from and what its secret was. The alchemist's name was Zelaznus.

Zelaznus was fascinated with the strange dust and spent several weeks trying to discover its properties. He found that the remote action of the dust worked even when the two piles were over a hundred feet apart—even when buildings were in between them. Zelaznus also found impurities in the dust—a reddish powder that indicated the sample came from somewhere in the Feldspaal Mountains. Before he had been able to discover any more, however, a warrant was issued for Brand's capture on several counts of theft from public officials. Brand fled the city, traveling through Peraltia to Feldspaal. After several months of searching, he found the mine where the dwarves had uncovered the strange mineral. The dwarves considered the mineral to be a curiosity of no particular importance; they had given some of it to human emissaries, knowing that humans tended to be fascinated by natural oddities (the dwarves being, in general, a far more practical people).

Brand suspected that the dust had the potential to serve a purpose much more valuable than the entertainment of idle nobles, but the zelaznium (as it would come to be called) was rare and nobody was mining it—the dwarves had only found a few tiny pockets of it while looking for veins of iron. Brand had quite a stash of gold socked away from his pickpocketing days—he had never planned on being a thief forever—but he didn't have enough to pay the dwarves to begin mining for the mineral in earnest. He bought all the zelaznium the dwarves had (which fit easily in his backpack) and then took a huge gamble: he traveled deep into the Thick Forest to meet the elves, demanding his inheritance as a pretext for getting their help to uncover the secrets of the strange mineral. The elves agreed to send three of their most knowledgeable craftsmen with Brand. Being a wanted man in Avaress and needing secrecy for his experiments (lest someone else start mining zelaznium, increasing the demand and raising the price), Brand and the three elves made their way across the Wastes of Preel and set up shop in the valley now known as Brandsveid. At first any practical use for the magical properties of zelaznium eluded them, but they found that the metallurgical properties of the mineral were astounding: adding a small amount to steel made it far stronger, resistant to rust, and able to keep an edge. Brand began selling swords to anyone who would buy them. The swords were of only average crafts-manship—elves not being the best blacksmiths—but the quality of the steel made them more than a match for most blades. Eventually Brand had made enough money to hire dwarven craftsmen to forge the blades.

The elves and dwarves did not at first work very well together. They spoke different languages and evinced the mutual antipathy that was typical between the two races. Additionally, the elves were trying to move on to creating something with zelaznium that was not a weapon and they didn't appreciate being interrupted with questions about swordmaking. It was this combination of miscommunication, general confusion, and outright hostility that resulted in the Seven Blades of Brakboorn—Brakboorn being an ancient Dwarvish word meaning something like "colossal screwup."

But the Blades of Brakboorn turned out better than anyone expected. The dwarf who had forged them realized that the proportions of iron, carbon, chrome, and zelaznium were off when he saw that he had misread instructions that had been written using Elvish numerals. As soon as the blades were cool, he lay one across an anvil and struck it with a hammer, thinking it would shatter and he could reuse the metal for something else. But the blade wouldn't shatter. Nor would it bend without great exertion, and the blade would snap completely straight as soon as he took his weight off it. Further experiments showed that the blades wouldn't rust and could slice though bricks without dulling.

Brand discovered that the blades possessed an even more remarkable property: when one blade was pointed at another, it acted like one of Milah's mirrors, reflecting the surroundings of the other mirror rather than its own. Brand obsessed with trying to find a practical purpose for the swords, and finally came up with one: by distributing them to some of the most powerful men in the Six Kingdoms—and holding onto one himself—he could receive glimpses of what was happening across the land of Dis. Of course, the holders of the other swords would have this power as well, so he ordered the dwarves to deface the blades with Elvish characters. When they were done, it was nearly impossible to see that the sword was sometimes reflecting events from hundreds of miles away. Only Brand's sword, Orthslaagt, was allowed to keep its mirror-like sheen.

Brand traveled the Six Kingdoms with the swords, giving one to each king—or, when more practical, the prince who was most likely to become king. Most of the recipients were at first skeptical, but were won over by the obvious superiority of the blades. Boric had been the recipient of the last of the six, Brakslaagt.

After giving him Brakslaagt, Brand followed Boric to Brobdingdon, having heard that there was a possibility of a Peraltia-Ytrisk alliance forged through Boric's marriage of Urgulana. He witnessed the ceremony—and more importantly, Boric's public rejection of Milah. Brand suspected that Milah was the daughter of Zelaznus (she was only a little girl when Brand came to Zelasnus's laboratory years earlier), and that the mirrors she carried were infused with zelaznium. He approached her after her rejection and offered her a job. She traveled with him back to his workshop and soon they were married. A few months later she gave birth to Leto, whom she knew was Boric's child, and they raised the boy together.

Brand's workmen produced many more swords but were never able to replicate the Blades of Brakslaagt. Still, they made a hefty profit selling swords to the noblemen of the Six Kingdoms. Brand was proud to learn very recently that the sword Clovis had used to slay the Dragon of Kalvan was one of their making.

"*I* killed the dragon!" Boric growled in response to this. "The dragon just happened to fall on Clovis's sword."

"Well, then I suppose Brakslaagt deserves some of the credit as well," agreed Brand.

"Brakslaagt!" Boric hissed. "A man is more than his sword!"

Brand nodded, smiling. "Well said, Boric."

"So you're just a businessman, is that it?" asked Boric. "You have no plans to conquer all of Dis? You're just a well-meaning guy who has five walking corpses who do your bidding. And the goblin army, that's just to give the goblins something to do, right?"

"It does keep the goblins out of trouble," Brand said. "But I'm afraid the army is going to serve another purpose soon."

"Aha!" Boric exclaimed. "You *are* planning an attack! Where? Quirin? Peraltia?"

Brand shook his head grimly. "We're not attacking anyone," he said. "We're *being* attacked."

"Attacked?" Boric asked. "By whom? Who would traverse the Wastes of Preel or the Vast Desert to attack you?"

Brand sighed. "The combined armies of the Six Kingdoms of Dis."

# Twenty-Five

Boric stood on the balcony of the room at the top of Kra'al Brand-skelt looking across the valley toward the small watchtower guarding the Salarat Pass. Beyond the pass, extending as far as Boric could see into the Wastes of Preel, was what looked like an undulating sea flecked with tiny colorful dots—the banners of the Six Kingdoms of Dis. There was the yellow-and-black banner of the desert kingdom of Quirin; the red banner of Blinsk; the golden banner of Avaress; the green-and-blue banner of Peraltia; the silver banner of Skaal; and right up in front, the blue-and-white banner of Ytrisk. Somewhere down there was that treacherous coward Yoric. The Six Kingdoms of Dis, which never agreed on anything, had combined their armies to wage war on Brand.

"I can't believe that Yoric has aligned himself with the Skaal," said Boric. "They've been our mortal enemies for decades."

Brand replied, "My spies tell me that just after your death Yoric received ambassadors from Skaal and Avaress who convinced him of the threat of my new kingdom. He signed a truce with Skaal declaring peace between the two kingdoms until the supposed threat of Brandsveid is dealt with. I'm sure they'll be back at each other's throats once I'm dead."

"But why send their armies here to kill you?" asked Boric. "I mean, I obviously have my own reasons for wanting to kill you, but what do the rulers of the Six Kingdoms have against you? I thought you said noblemen in most of the kingdoms had bought mirrors from you."

"Oh, yes, individually they are all big fans of our work. They love to be able to spy on their neighbors and communicate with their troops over long distances. But they aren't so big on their neighbors being able to better spy on *them* and communicate with *their* troops over long distances. They feel that they are shelling out a lot of money for no net gain."

"Hmm," said Boric. "Perhaps they have a point."

"Absolutely," said Brand. "They pay good money for an advantage over their rivals but they get nowhere, because their rivals are paying for the same advantage. But that's the problem with running a kingdom in Dis, Boric, as you well know. When you're constantly at war or under the threat of war with all your neighbors, every gain is someone else's loss. That's not the fault of the mirrors; it's the fault of the idiotic way the kingdoms are run. I mean, look at those armies, Boric! Imagine if such a spirit of unity could be invoked for peace! But no, the only thing they can agree on is that my enterprise needs to be destroyed."

"I don't buy it," said Boric. "They sent their armies marching across the Wastes because they think they're paying too much for their mirrors?"

"Oh, no," Brand said. "I mean, that's part of it. But mostly it's just fear."

"Of your goblin army?"

Brand laughed. "No. My goblin army is no threat and they know it. What they are afraid of is the change that the mirrors will bring— the change they're already bringing. You see, merchants are different from kings. Merchants thrive on information—what their customers want, how much they want, how much they're willing to pay for it, how much is left in the warehouse, what the weather is like where they are headed, and on and on. Merchants can use the mirrors to run their business better and make more money than they did before—and yes, some of that is at the expense of other merchants, but *not all of it*. Merchants can actually *create* value, whereas kings can only steal it."

Boric wasn't following. "What do you mean, create value?"

"It's complicated," said Brand. "You kings tend to think in terms of gold. Gold coming in is good. Gold going out is bad. But the reality is much more complicated than that. Like these mirrors, for example. You might trade a thousand gold pieces for a pair of our mirrors and be happy you did it, because you need the mirrors more than you need the gold. But I'm happy too because I need the gold more than I need the mirrors. So in a sense, we both end up with more than we started out with. Just by trading one thing for another, we've *created value*. And the chief benefactor of the value that's being created in Dis is the merchants."

It was clear that Boric still didn't get it.

"Never mind," said Brand. "Suffice it to say that merchants are becoming more wealthy and powerful in Dis. Part of that is the mirrors, but the process has been going on for some time. Because the kings believe that there can't be winners without losers, they feel threatened by the rise of the merchants, and they attribute that rise to me. They think that they can hold onto power a little longer by wiping me out. And they're probably right. If they destroy my operation here, confiscate all the mirrors, make it illegal for the merchants to possess them…they could set back progress in Dis for a long time. Keep people poor, send the excess population off to die in pointless wars, keep all the wealth for themselves…but then, I know you understand how *that* works."

Boric did understand. And up until two and a half weeks ago, he had been one of the prime instigators. He had always told himself it was because there was no better way, that this was just how things were. But of course it was convenient for him to think so, wasn't it? And it wasn't like he had ever *tried* to find a better way. The one time a really great idea had been presented to him—Milah's mirrors—he had rejected it out of hand. How much better off might Ytrisk be now if he had backed her up rather than sending her away? Boric had been far more concerned with his own comfort than with the good of his citizens. How many men had died so that he could have the Warmest Coat in Ytrisk? There was no doubt in Boric's mind that if he hadn't been killed that day, he would right now be leading the Ytriskian army against Brand.

Truth be told, he still kind of wanted to kill Brand. It *was* his fault that Boric was a wraith, even if the creation of the Seven Blades of Brakboorn had been an accident. But maybe if Brand remained alive, he'd be able to find a way to break the curse of the Blades. That is, assuming he actually wanted to.

"So what happens when you die?" asked Boric. "Do you become a wraith as well?"

Brand shrugged. "I guess we'll find out soon enough. My scouts say the last of the Ytriskian and Skaal regiments will arrive tomorrow. I suspect the attack will begin not long after."

"If you become a wraith, I suppose you'll be a bit more motivated to break the enchantment," said Boric.

"At first, I suppose," replied Brand. "But as you know, the motivations of the living tend to fade after a few years as a wraith. The other wraiths, who died years before you, are just shadows of their former selves. They do nothing that I don't specifically order them to do. They no longer have any wills of their own."

"Years?" Boric asked. "You think it will take that long?"

"I have no idea, Boric! I know you don't believe me, but I've been trying to solve the riddle of the curse since Loren showed up here ten years ago. How much longer will it take after the kings of Dis destroy my workroom and slaughter my craftsmen? Who knows? A hundred years? A thousand? We'll all just be shadows by then, envying the merciful fates of Milah and Leto."

Boric winced at the thought. Leto, having received word of the pending invasion, had returned to Brandsveid and was now overseeing the castle fortifications. Boric had observed him for some time and concluded that Milah was right: Leto possessed a rare gift of being able to assess a situation and see exactly how to address it. Leto had commandeered the elves and dwarves from the workroom and put them to work distributing precisely organized caches of weapons around the castle, including pots of oil that could be heated on portable stoves to be thrown onto attackers below, as well as buttressing gates with steel bars and making dozens of other preparations. It was too bad it was all for naught: there was no way Kra'al Brandskelt could repel a full assault by the combined armies of the Six Kingdoms. Leto, Milah, Brand, and everyone else in the castle would be captured or killed.

And Brand was right: as bad as his situation was now, it would only be made worse by the death of Brand and the taking of Kra'al Brandskelt. The workroom would be destroyed and the craftsmen killed or scattered. Most likely, once the kings had secured a monopoly over the mirrors, they would outlaw any further research into the properties of zelaznium—dooming Boric to be a wraith forever. And if Brand stood by and allowed Milah and Leto to die, after everything he had learned, then he truly was a monster.

"That's not going to happen," said Boric.

"What do you mean?" asked Brand. "We can't withstand an assault by the Six Armies."

"Maybe not," said Boric. "But we're going to give it a shot. I need schematics of the castle, a map of Brandsveid, and a list of all your tactical units and their commanders."

"What are you planning to do?" asked Brand.

"I may not know much about economics," said Boric, "but I know how to make the taking of Kra'al Brandskelt a lot more expensive."

# Twenty-Six

There aren't many meetings more awkward than one between a man who has been dead for more than two weeks and the son he never knew he had. There was no time to stand on ceremony, however—whatever ceremony might have applied in this instance. Boric needed Leto's help to prepare the troops and Kra'al Brandskelt for the attack. Brand and Leto had taken some precautionary measures before the current crisis, of course, but they needed a more specific tactical plan if they were going to survive the onslaught of the Six Armies. Boric had an idea for such a plan, and if it were correctly implemented he put the odds of its success at about fifty-fifty. Failure would result in complete and utter defeat and most likely the deaths of Brand, Leto, and Milah. He left that part out when he explained the plan.

Leto accepted his responsibilities with good humor; Milah had evidently informed him that Boric hadn't intentionally abandoned him nor knowingly allowed Leto's grandmother to be exiled. In any case, Leto didn't seem to be the sort to allow personal grudges to get in the way of what needed to be done. He understood that Boric knew more about warfare than anyone else in Kra'al Brandskelt, and he did what Boric asked him to do, only occasionally challenging him on points where his own expertise was greater than Boric's.

The other wraiths who had been pursuing Boric had returned from the west, but none of them were much help with the preparations. It pained Boric to see once-mighty kings reduced to a purely servile role, but the wraiths simply didn't have enough humanity left in them to think independently. Corbet, one of the longest dead, was the worst off: he hovered near Brand almost constantly, just waiting to be given some task to perform, but the others weren't much better. Loren of Avaress—the one who had been mauled by a boar—tended to hang out in dark corners of the castle moping and scaring the living daylights out of the servants until he was ordered to do something more constructive. Garamond of Peraltia and Djibalti of Quirin spent their days roaming the castle grounds, skewering mice and other vermin with their enchanted swords, which at least kept them out of trouble. Skerritt of Blinsk, who had died three years before Boric, was evidently still considered the "new guy" by the other wraiths; he hung around Boric like a puppy starved for affection, occasionally handing him random objects like a candlestick or spool of yarn in an attempt to anticipate Boric's needs. Boric finally sent him on a quest to retrieve half a dozen objects that he highly doubted could be found anywhere in Kra'al Brandskelt, and Skerritt stunned him by returning two hours later bearing a soapstone figurine of an elephant, a raven's claw, a bag of pumpkin seeds, a beaver trap, and a pineapple. Fortunately by this time Boric's preparations were all but complete.

The attack started two days after their preparations began, just before dawn. The kings knew that goblins and ogres saw better at night than by day, and they were determined to take full advantage of the daylight. Brand's forces were vastly outnumbered but they possessed one big advantage: the ring of nearly impenetrable mountains around Brandsveid. There was only one place an army could get through: Salarat Pass. The narrowest point of this pass was blocked by a massive gate built of pine timbers and reinforced with steel bands. Overlooking the gate on each side were twin guard towers the goblins called the Fangs of Salarat.

The assault began, as expected, with the huge battering ram that the army had been assembling for two days on the plain. It consisted of a wooden frame from which a massive pine timber was suspended by chains. The frame was covered with animal skins that had been drenched with water to protect the assembly from fire or arrows from above. The head of the ram was encased in a steel cap, and steel bands encircled the rest of the shaft every few feet. Boric could only imagine what it was like to drag that thing across the Wastes of Preel; it had to weigh four tons. Boric had watched as men struggled all night to pull the huge contraption into place, its large wooden wheels being of little use on the rocky, uneven ground. Mercifully, most of the men didn't have to struggle long: they were constantly being skewered by goblin archers hiding in the rocks above and being replaced by fresh recruits from behind. By the time the ram was at the gate, Salarat Pass was slick with the blood of men whose bodies had been dragged back to the plain. Presumably the bodies would have been left to rot had they not been an obstacle to advancing forces.

Boric had been watching from the eastern tower, but as the ram approached the gate he retreated across the valley floor to Kra'al Brandskelt. It wasn't the ram he feared, but rather the approaching daylight. As he strode across the valley, he heard the booming of the ram striking the gate echoing from the mountains. He had planned as well as he could; now it was up to the goblins manning the Fangs to hold the army at the gate. He disappeared into the castle as the first rays of morning pierced the horizon.

Boric received reports of the status of the assault throughout the day. By midmorning, the ram had splintered the gate. By noon, a small force of armored Avaressian knights had broken through the breach and was massacred in short order by goblins waiting inside. Meanwhile, men with axes and pry bars continued to work on the gates, trying to widen the breach. This was evidently the job given to the more expendable of the troops: the average lifespan of a member of the demolition crew was about forty-five seconds—and that included the walk to the gate.

Inside the gate waited a ring of several thousand of the most disciplined goblins Brand's army had to offer. They were still goblins, of course, so there was little question that they would rout and run to the hills if the battle started to turn against them, but as long as the odds were in their favor, they made for a formidable fighting force. Several hundred yards behind them stood the bulk of the goblin army, forming a barrier in front of Kra'al Brandskelt. This last line of defense backed right up against the moat surrounding the castle, partly because the ground sloped upward toward the castle and Boric wanted the advancing humans to see the full goblin army on display—but also partly because it gave the goblins no place to run. If the human armies got past the defensive line at the gate, these goblins would be forced to fight to the last man. He hoped it didn't come to that.

Several times it nearly did. The breach in the gate had been widened enough that it was impossible for the goblin archers to stop all the soldiers pouring through, which meant that the goblins inside were forced to fight pitched battles. Wave after wave of human soldiers poured in, and each time they were slaughtered or beaten back by the goblins. By late afternoon, the goblins were exhausted and Boric had to order them relieved by a less disciplined unit from the main force. Boric was all but certain that the goblins would rout, but they were eager to prove themselves and more than a little enthusiastic about the idea of finally having a chance to kill some humans, and the line held. Just after sundown, three sharp notes were sounded from a horn atop Kra'al Brandskelt. The goblins turned and ran.

The human armies, momentarily startled at the sudden retreat, nevertheless pressed onward, thousands of men pouring through the gap, moving at double-time in the dim light toward the goblin army awaiting them in front of Kra'al Brandskelt. Except the army wasn't there.

The first hundred or so men plunged headlong into the moat, and it was only the agonized screams of those who somehow survived that finally halted the advance. Mass confusion ensued. Where had the goblin army gone?

In point of fact, most of the goblin army had been gone for some time. Only the first few rows of the army had been composed of actual goblins, and these had fled into the hills as soon as the horn sounded. The human force, composed of regiments from Quirin, Skaal, and Peraltia, faced an army of helmets on pikes. The remainder of the human army waited outside the gates, not wanting to send their whole force in at once. Word that it was a trap spread rapidly through the ranks, but the human commanders inside Brandsveid insisted on carrying the plan through to completion. Engineers were sent forward with a folding bridge that could be thrown over the moat and soldiers ran across it, encountering no resistance. A smaller ram, composed only of a pine timber with metal handles affixed to it, was carried across the bridge, and the men set about breaking down the gate to the castle.

Meanwhile, the dozen ogres that were in Brand's employ began throwing stones and fallen trees down from the hills on either side of the Fangs, crushing anyone unlucky enough to be underneath. Half of the human army—the Avaressian, Blinskian, and Ytriskian contingents—retreated to the plain while the other half waited nervously inside. Soon the pass was hopelessly blocked: men could still crawl through the debris one by one—and those who tried were quickly put down by goblin archers—but a mass retreat from within was impossible.

The humans inside the gate, nearly blind in the gathering darkness, were now beset by a horrendous cacophony of wailing from the hills around them. The sound, echoing off the mountain-side, seemed to come from everywhere at once. Many of the men panicked, pushing forward onto the bridge and knocking several dozen into the moat. The crush of men at the gate made it impossible to maneuver the ram, so there was no escape, even into the castle.

The officers of the attacking force had done their best to order the men into a defensive circle, but the darkness, general confusion, and panic rendered the men into a sort of undulating, vaguely pear-shaped formation. Before discipline could be restored, the attack began.

Goblins poured out of the hills, executing quick hit-and-run attacks against the human army. Mostly these were an annoyance rather than a true threat: the goblins didn't stick around long enough to do much serious damage. More worrying were the figures in black who moved in silence and carried blades that sliced through chainmail as if it were paper. These mysterious warriors fought tirelessly, cutting down a man with nearly every swing, and they seemed impervious to attack. The dark specters also fought in hit-and-run fashion, adding to the overall terror of the situation. When an attacker burst from the darkness, it was often difficult to tell at first whether it was a goblin or one of the lethal and unstoppable warriors. The men fought bravely, but after several hours of harassment they were exhausted and greatly diminished in numbers, whereas the wraiths and goblins kept coming with no sign of ever stopping—or even slowing. The officers urged the men to hold out until morning when they would be able to see the goblins coming and perhaps the wraiths would weaken, but there was no hope of that. About two hours before dawn, the human army threw down its arms and surrendered. Of the twenty thousand or so men that had broken through the gate, perhaps two-thirds survived, and many of those were badly wounded.

Boric recalled the wraiths and issued an order to the goblins to clear the humans from the bridge and disarm the army. The bridge was clear in short order, and Boric made his way across to reenter the castle, wanting to get a view of the battlefield from above. Brand came up alongside him, with Corbet the wraith close behind.

"What are you doing?" Brand demanded, gripping Boric by the arm.

"Accepting the enemy's surrender," answered Boric.

"There can be no surrender!" Brand shouted. "If we don't stop them now, they will keep coming. In a month, or a year, or five years, the armies of the Six Kingdoms will be back, stronger than before—and they aren't likely to fall for your parlor tricks again."

Boric turned to face Brand. "You, a peddler of magic mirrors, are accusing me of parlor tricks. That ruse, Your Lordship, was an example of *tactics*. Unhand me."

Brand let go of Boric's arm. "I command you to finish this," he said evenly.

Boric laughed his harsh, rasping laugh. "You've been hanging out with sycophantic corpses too long," he said. "I might get there eventually, but I'm not there yet. I didn't fight this battle for you. I fought it for Milah and Leto—and for me. These men surrendered, and the honorable thing to do is to disarm them and send them home."

"Honorable!" exclaimed Brand. "What do you know of honor, Slaagtghast? You're a wraith."

Boric turned and continued walking toward the castle.

"Fine," said Brand. "I'll finish the job. Vektghast, guard the bridge."

Boric stopped, turning to face them. Brand turned and walked away. Corbet remained behind, drawing his sword. Boric turned to face Corbet, and Corbet strode toward him.

Boric took a swipe at Corbet's feet, which Corbet easily parried. Corbet stabbed at midsection and Boric swept it aside. The two wraiths continued to strike and parry for a minute, and it soon became clear that Corbet had improved greatly since Boric and he had last met. He must have stepped up his training at Kra'al Skaal after his humbling encounter with Boric. After all, he couldn't have become a great swordsman *after* he died, could he? How could a dead man's reflexes be improved? No, Boric determined, Corbet could only be as good as he was when he died, no better. As Brand had said, the wraiths were only shadows of their former selves.

That gave Boric an idea: there was little initiative or creativity left in Corbet; he could only do what Brand—or his own reflexes and training—told him to do. He fought well but mechanically, using all the same thrusts and maneuvers he had used when he was alive. But he wasn't alive anymore—and neither was Boric.

Boric deliberately left himself open for a blow and Corbet predictably took advantage of the opportunity, thrusting his sword deep into Boric's sternum. If Boric had been alive, it would have been a death blow. The enchanted blade did sting a bit as it sliced through what was left of his vitals, but it couldn't kill him. The thrust put Corbet off balance and dangerously close to Boric. Grabbing Corbet's wrist and twisting to the right, Boric caused him to stumble toward the edge of the bridge. Boric leaned forward and thrust his foot hard against Corbet's desiccated gut. It crunched like a pile of dead leaves as Corbet stumbled backward, falling off the bridge into the abyss below. There was a momentary, ghastly howl as Corbet fell—and then silence.

"Brand!" called Boric, striding across the bridge.

But Brand was already on the other side of the moat, moving quickly to where the other wraiths had gathered. Presumably he intended to seek protection from Boric among the wraiths. But someone barred his way: Milah, who had been hiding in the hills, had come down to confront him.

"What are you doing, Brand? Why was Boric fighting Corbet on the bridge?"

"I gave Boric an order and he refused it," said Brand.

"I don't work for you, elf-boy," Boric said, advancing toward them, his sword still drawn. "You want a job finished, Brand? I'll finish the job I came here to do."

"What's he talking about, Brand? What job do you want him to finish?"

"He wants to massacre the prisoners," said Boric.

"Brand, that's idiotic," said Milah.

"I was going to go with cowardly and evil, but yeah, idiotic is good too," said Boric.

"These prisoners are our leverage," said Milah. "If we kill them, we've got another twenty thousand men out there just waiting to get revenge. How long do you think a few fallen trees are going to keep them out? If you kill these men, you kill us all."

Brand was speechless. "I...didn't think..."

"Yeah, you can stop there," said Boric, sheathing his sword. He walked over to a goblin captain who was coordinating the disarming of the soldiers. "Once you've finished disarming them, set up a tent over there for wounded men who need medical attention. Let them tend their own wounded, but give them whatever supplies they need. The unwounded should be separated into two groups: the nobles and the commoners. Put the nobles here and the commoners over there. And I want a full head count of each."

"How do I know who is what?" asked the goblin, confused.

"Anybody wearing any shiny armor goes over here. If you're in doubt, assume it's a nobleman. Got it?"

The goblin saluted and repeated the orders to a group of his subordinates. It took about an hour for the disarming and separating. Roughly one in twenty men stood in the nobles group. Boric walked among them, looking for faces he recognized. The men recoiled in terror, recognizing him as one of the dark warriors who had dismembered so many of their men. Part of their horror may have been due to the fact that he had been slashed and stabbed several dozen times in the course of the battle; he looked like a ragdoll that had been chewed up by a rabid dog and smelled like a side of beef about two weeks past its prime.

Boric recognized King Balinn of Quirin, King Sharvek of Skaal, and King Gavin of Peraltia among the nobles. Gavin had a bad gash in his right leg, but had remained with the unwounded to allow the worse off to be treated first. Toward the back of the group Boric saw a young Ytriskian knight he recognized. "You," he said, pointing to the knight, "come with me."

The man was clearly frightened but followed Boric without comment. When they were sufficiently distant from the group, Boric turned and spoke to him. "I need you to deliver a message to your fellows outside the gate. Tell them we have fourteen thousand three hundred ninety-one men in captivity. They will be well-treated as long as no attempt is made to attack us or rescue them. For every man that you send through the pass, we will execute one prisoner, starting with King Gavin of Peraltia and working our way down the chain of command. Brand will meet with your commanders on the plain tomorrow at dusk to negotiate the terms of your surrender." Boric had the man repeat the message back, which he did flawlessly.

Boric beckoned to the goblin captain he had addressed earlier. "Take ten of your best men and escort this man through the Pass of Salarat. Instruct the captain of the archers he is not to be harmed. Go!"

Boric turned back to Brand. "This sort of trade I understand," he said. "They want their men alive more than we want to kill them. Win-win."

Brand gave a pained smile, and Boric retreated to the castle in anticipation of the sunrise.

Not two hours after the knight left with the message, a cadre of goblins came down from the hills with two human spies who had been sent to gather information on the situation inside Brandsveid. Boric had been prepared for this. He had the spies wait in the foyer of Kra'al Brandskelt and ordered a pair of goblins to retrieve King Gavin from outside. The goblins returned with Gavin between them. Gavin's boot had been removed and his leg was wrapped with blood-soaked bandages. His face was pale, and he could barely walk, but he held his head high as he limped through the foyer past the spies, disappearing into the dark room in which Boric had ensconced himself. The goblins entered behind him closing the door. There was a scream and then silence. A moment later, the goblins exited the room, one of them holding a severed hand on a plate. The middle finger was adorned with Gavin's emerald ring.

The goblins slid the hand into a burlap sack and handed it to one of the spies. "Master says take this to your king. And he says King Sharvek of Skaal is next." The goblins escorted the terrified man outside, and Boric stepped into the foyer. "Put the other one with the commoners," he ordered another goblin. When the goblin had left, Boric said to another, "Find me a nurse. Gavin's leg needs attention. And when you're done with that, get me another hand from one of the corpses. Somebody fat and hairy like Sharvek. Just in case they need more convincing not to mess with us."

No further convincing was necessary.

# Twenty-Seven

Just after sundown the next day, Boric, Brand, and Leto climbed over the pile of debris blocking Salarat Pass and walked out onto the plain where a circle of torches blazed. Inside the circle a table and chairs had been set up. Seated on the far side were the kings of Avaress, Blinsk, and Ytrisk. Yoric sat in the middle, with King Rapelini of Avaress on his right and King Jeddac of Blinsk on his left. Four knights stood guard on the edges of the circle.

Yoric got to his feet as the three approached. "I demand you release our men," snapped Yoric. "Taking hostages is a violation of the Code of Nobles."

"So is attacking a peaceful country," said Brand.

Yoric continued undeterred, "And I demand that you dismiss this... *thing* from our midst." He was glaring disgustedly at Boric.

"I don't believe it's up to you to determine the makeup of my delegation, Your Highness," said Brand. "Now if you would be so kind as to sit, we can discuss how we are going to resolve this unfortunate situation."

Yoric, grumbling, sat down, and Boric, Brand, and Leto sat across from the three kings. Boric had replaced his cloak—again—and done his best to repair his wrappings, but he couldn't blame Yoric for taking offense at his presence. He looked like a badly designed scarecrow and, thanks to Milah pouring an entire bottle of perfume over his head, smelled of wildflowers and death. He had given up trying to swat the flies that buzzed around his head.

Brand cleared his throat and began, "The Kingdom of Brandsveid condemns without qualification the unjust and immoral assault on its sovereign territory by the—"

"For Grovlik's sake," grumbled Jeddac. "What do you want in exchange for releasing our men?"

"We have three demands," said Brand, who seemed relieved to be able to cut out the formalities; his eyes were watering from Boric's stench. "First, you withdraw all of your troops back to their own respective kingdoms. Second, you pledge never to mount another attack on Brandsveid as long as our armed forces remain inside Salarat Pass. Third…" Brand paused to scowl at Boric, who nodded almost imperceptibly. "Third, we demand that Yoric confess to the murder of King Boric, abdicate the throne of Ytrisk, and hand himself over to the legitimate King of Ytrisk to be sentenced for his crimes."

Jeddac gasped and Rapelini's mouth fell open. "This is outrageous!" bellowed Yoric. "I had nothing to do with Boric's death. And I am king because Boric's own will named me as his successor."

"That will is a forgery," said Brand. "This one is genuine." He produced from within his cloak a rolled-up sheet of paper bearing Boric's seal, which he showed to the three kings. He handed the paper to King Jeddac, who broke the seal and began reading.

"I, Boric son of Toric, being of sound mind and body, yadda yadda yadda…okay, here we go: I name as my successor to the throne of Ytrisk, my son by Milah of Avaress, Leto. Leto is a very intelligent, hardworking young man with a bright future ahead of him. I believe he will make an excellent king."

"Who in Varnoth's name is Leto?" growled Yoric.

"That would be me," said Leto. "I suggest you keep reading."

Jeddac frowned at the paper. "That's all there is to…oh, wait. 'P.S.: If I am stabbed in the back by that coward Randor, my murderous brother Yoric is responsible. P.P.S.: Yoric may try to fool you with a forged will. Don't fall for it. This is the real one.'"

"As you can see," said Brand, "it's dated the very day that Boric died. It's witnessed by me and the kings of Skaal, Peraltia, and Quirin."

"This is absurd," Yoric protested. "Boric couldn't possibly have met with those three kings the day he died. They were hundreds of miles away! And how convenient that this will was supposedly witnessed by the very same kings that you now have in captivity. You probably put them on the rack until they agreed to sign."

"I assure you," Brand said with a smile, "no torture was necessary. You may just have to accept the fact that your fellow kings don't like you very much, Yoric."

"You see?" said Yoric. "He's practically admitting that this will is a forgery! And although you may have secured the signatures of the other three kings under duress, I can tell you for certain that Boric's signature is forged. The loops on the 'B' are all wrong."

"Really?" asked Brand, taking the will from Jeddac and studying it intently. He held it in front of Boric. "What do you think?"

"Looks real to me," said Boric.

"And how would *you* know, wraith?" growled Yoric.

Boric pulled back his hood and carefully unwound the wrappings covering his face. The three kings recoiled in horror at what they saw.

"Because I'm Boric," he said, his rotten flesh contorting into a horrific grin.

Jeddac and Rapelini agreed to the terms.

# Twenty-Eight

Boric stood once again on the balcony of the top level of Kra'al Brandskelt as the first light of dawn gathered above the mountains to the east. The armies of the Six Kingdoms were retreating across the Wastes of Preel toward their homes. Among them was the newest king, Leto. Yoric was in chains in a wagon at the rear of the convoy.

"You did it, Boric," said Milah, coming up behind him. "You made peace between Brandsveid and the Six Kingdoms."

Boric nodded wearily.

"Brand isn't too thrilled that you've made Leto King of Ytrisk, though."

"He'll get over it," said Boric. "It's good for him to have a little friendly competition. Anyway, I owed it to Leto. And to the people of Ytrisk. He'll be a good king. He promised me that his first official action as king would be to revoke the proclamation of exile against the Witch…that is, against his grandmother, Anna."

"You've done something remarkable, Boric," said Milah. "You've opened up the possibility of a bright new future for the Land of Dis."

Boric peered into the glow on the horizon. "Too bright for me, I'm afraid."

"We'll find a cure, Boric. A way to break the enchantment."

Boric shook his head. "I've already found the cure," he said.

"What? How?"

Boric turned to face her. "Your husband, Brand, he's not a bad guy," said Boric. "But he needs to be careful, or he's going to turn into the very thing he hates. You need to watch him, make sure he does the right thing."

"I'm not following you, Boric."

"He wanted to slaughter all those people, Milah. After going on about how there were better ways to solve problems than violence, he wanted nothing more than to obliterate any threat to his regime. And frankly, I kind of wanted to kill them all too. I only stopped him because it seemed counterproductive. And cowardly."

"So Boric the Implacable has become a believer in peace?" Milah teased.

"I'm not sure I'm a believer in much of anything anymore. I've just become a lot less enthusiastic about killing things."

"Disenchanted," said Milah.

"Yeah," said Boric, stepping toward the half wall separating him from the abyss below. "I need you to give Brand a message for me," he said.

"Of course," replied Milah. "But why don't you just…"

"Tell him that the sword isn't holding onto him. He is holding onto the sword."

With that, Boric drew Brakslaagt one last time. He held it for a moment over the wall and then released his grip. The sword fell from his hand and disappeared into the abyss. Boric turned away as the first rays of the sun shot across the eastern sky.

"Good-bye, Milah," he said, and fell to the stone floor, dead.

# Twenty-Nine

Boric never felt his body strike the stone floor, but he did hear the distant beating of wings: Viriana the Eytrith had returned on her faithful steed Bubbles the wyndbahr. Boric got to his feet, ignoring Milah sobbing over his inanimate corpse, and walked to meet Bubbles as he alighted on the balcony.

"Hey there, boy," said Boric, rubbing the giant animal under its chin. "Good to see you." Bubbles licked Boric's face excitedly.

Viriana slid off the wyndbahr's back.

"Good to see you too," said Boric to Viriana. He was struck again by her beauty; she was, in her own way, as beautiful as Milah had been twenty years earlier. And Viriana's blond tresses always had that fetching windblown look, like she had just gotten off the back of a wyndbahr. He continued, "I'm a little surprised you bothered to come back. I imagine I've slipped a few notches in the rankings, what with sparing the lives of prisoners, letting the Six Armies escape, and throwing away my sword. I guess I'm just not cut out to drink mead with the likes of Hollick the Goblin-Slayer."

"No, I suppose not," she said.

"So where are you taking me? Not the Hall of Avandoor, surely. Some afterlife equivalent of the little kids' table?"

Viriana laughed. "Boric, let me explain something to you about the Halls of Avandoor. You're familiar with Grovlik and Magartha, right?"

"Of course," said Boric. "Grovlik is the great father-god who created the land of Dis. Magartha is his wife, goddess of living things."

"And what do you know of Kirilan?"

"The land of the dead? As much as anyone, I suppose. It is said to be a dark, shadowy land where the spirits of the dead roam aimlessly forever. Except for the greatest warriors, who are allowed to partake in the eternal feast in Avandoor."

"Yeah, not exactly," said Viriana. "I'll tell you the real story." She began:

"Grovlik created Dis, and Magartha filled it with living creatures. But shortly after she filled Dis with life, Magartha's creations began to die. This didn't particularly bother Grovlik; he pointed out that new creatures were being born all the time to replace the ones that died. He figured that everything balanced out. But Magartha was saddened by death—particularly the death of human beings, who had such short lifespans to begin with. She created a new land, an even better land than Dis, called Kirilan, where the spirits of those who died could go after death. Some people—murderers and other scum—she didn't bother to resurrect, but anyone who had tried to live a good life was transported to Kirilan to be given another chance at happiness.

"But soon Magartha faced a problem: Kirilan was a bountiful land, where there was plenty for everyone. There was no need for warfare or fighting. So what to do with all the warriors who had died bravely in combat, men who were basically good-hearted but whose lives had been devoted to fighting and killing? Such men weren't content with a quiet life of gardening or fishing. Not only that, but they threatened to disrupt the idyllic existence of the other residents of Kirilan with their brawling and carousing.

"So Magartha in her wisdom built a great fortress on an island in the middle of the Kirilan Sea. The whole fortress was one gigantic banquet hall filled with the most wonderful food and drink imaginable. She filled the hall with all the great warriors who lived in Kirilan, telling them she was treating them to a feast in honor of their bravery and skill. As more great warriors died, she sent them to the banquet hall as well, and soon it was the most amazing gathering of warriors anyone had ever known. They regaled each other with their stories, each one attempting to outdo the last. The food and drink never gave out, so the banquet just went on and on. It's been going on now for over a thousand years."

"So all this time," Boric started, "I've been trying to get into…"

"A prison, yes," answered Viriana. "Avandoor is an ancient word meaning something like asylum. Don't get me wrong, the food really is first rate. And I suppose they have a good time, in their own way. Most of them probably never even think about trying to escape. And that's a good thing, because there *is* no escape. Even if they could get outside the castle, they're in the middle of a vast ocean, hundreds of miles from the nearest land."

"But how can they just keep eating and drinking forever, without ever, you know…"

"People exist in only in spiritual form on Kirilan," answered Viriana. "You don't have the same physical compulsions as you do here on Dis. Nor are there the same consequences. One can eat and drink constantly for years without ever getting completely full—or suffering a hangover. And before you ask: no, there are no women in Avandoor."

"None?" asked Boric. "What of the women warriors of legend, such as Iliana the Huntress?"

"Oh, there are female warriors," replied Viriana. "But women fight out of necessity, not bloodlust. They don't find it difficult to adapt to a peaceful life on Kirilan."

"Wow," said Boric, trying to take in all this new information. For his part, he had had enough fighting and killing. Sitting next to Hollick the Goblin-Slayer for all eternity now sounded like the worst punishment he could imagine. He wouldn't mind spending a few hundred years with Viriana, though.

"So then," Boric started, "if people don't have the same sort of compulsions on Kirilan, then I suppose they don't, you know…"

"Oh, we do," Viriana replied, smiling coyly. "Just not as a matter of compulsion. It's more like pure recreation."

"Oh," said Boric. Kirilan was sounding better by the minute. "So I, um…that is, do you have plans for dinner?"

"It depends," said Viriana. "Do you actually like mead?"

"Of course not," said Boric. "Horrible stuff."

"Good," replied Viriana. "Get on the wyndbahr, Boric. We're going for a ride."

# Acknowledgments

With thanks to Joel Bezaire, Colleen Diamond, Nicklaus Louis, Medeia Sharif, Michele Smith, Charity VanDeberg, and my lovely wife, Julia, for their support, comments, corrections, and suggestions.

# About the Author

Robert Kroese's sense of irony was honed growing up in Grand Rapids, Michigan— home of the Amway Corporation and the Gerald R. Ford Museum, and the first city in the United States to fluoridate its water supply. In second grade, he wrote his first novel, the saga of Captain Bill and his spaceship *Thee Eagle*. This turned out to be the high point of his academic career. After barely graduating from Calvin College in 1992 with a philosophy degree, he was fired from a variety of jobs before moving to California, where he stumbled into software development. As this job required neither punctuality nor a sense of direction, he excelled at it. In 2009, he called upon his extensive knowledge of useless information and love of explosions to write his first novel, *Mercury Falls*. Since then, he has written nine more novels and learned to play the guitar very poorly.

Email Rob at rob@robertkroese.com, find out about him at http://sfauthor.net, connect with him on Facebook at www.facebook.com/robkroese, and follow him on Twitter at www.twitter.com/robkroese. To get exclusive free fiction and updates about future releases from Robert Kroese, sign up for his mailing list at http://sfauthor.net/get-email-updates.

Made in the USA
Middletown, DE
20 July 2018